"It seems we have something to discuss."

"We do." Devlyn's heart pounded in her chest, but she faced Rye, wishing he didn't look so put together when she felt torn apart. "You need to leave. Whatever you're doing here, it has nothing to do with us, and I won't have you messing up our lives. You may have money and clout in Knoxville, and I'm sure that makes you happy, but no one and nothing is going to mess up my son's life. Especially not you."

"*Our* son."

The words cut her like a hot knife on butter.

"The son you kept hidden from me."

She rolled her eyes. "Hidden in plain sight, but you didn't bother to come to town, to come home, even to visit your grandmother or close up her house when she moved to Knoxville. We weren't hidden, Rye. We were right here, all the while. You just never bothered to check."

Multipublished bestselling author **Ruth Logan Herne** loves God, her country, her family, dogs, chocolate and coffee! Married to a very patient man, she lives in an old farmhouse in Upstate New York and thinks possums should leave the cat food alone and snakes should always live outside. There are no exceptions to either rule! Visit Ruth at ruthloganherne.com.

Books by Ruth Logan Herne

Love Inspired

Kendrick Creek

Rebuilding Her Life
The Path Not Taken

Golden Grove

A Hopeful Harvest
Learning to Trust
Finding Her Christmas Family

Shepherd's Crossing

Her Cowboy Reunion
A Cowboy in Shepherd's Crossing
Healing the Cowboy's Heart

Visit the Author Profile page
at Harlequin.com for more titles.

The Path Not Taken

Ruth Logan Herne

LOVE INSPIRED
INSPIRATIONAL ROMANCE

LOVE INSPIRED®
INSPIRATIONAL ROMANCE

Recycling programs
for this product may
not exist in your area.

ISBN-13: 978-1-335-40954-6

The Path Not Taken

This edition published by arrangement with Harlequin Books S.A.

For questions and comments about the quality of this book, please contact us at CustomerService@Harlequin.com.

Love Inspired
22 Adelaide St. West, 40th Floor
Toronto, Ontario M5H 4E3, Canada
www.Harlequin.com

Printed in U.S.A.

I say unto you, that likewise joy shall be
in heaven over one sinner that repenteth,
more than over ninety and nine just persons,
which need no repentance.

—*Luke* 15:7

This book is dedicated to my brother Sean,
who always sees beyond the obvious
with an amazing heart and an even better soul.
I love you, Sean! You mean the world to me.

Chapter One

Ryland Bauer wasn't driving to Kendrick Creek, Tennessee, just to negotiate a post-wildfire real estate deal for his successful Knoxville development company and get the project rolling.

He was on his way to a meeting he couldn't avoid because nestled in the middle of Smoky Mountain Development Corporation's "over 55" neighborhood concept was a thirteen-acre property owned by Devlyn McCabe. His first love. Maybe his only true love. No one before or since had touched his soul like Devlyn, but that was a long time ago.

He swallowed a sigh, determined to think of something else. Anything else. The land. The project. But there was no separating the project from Devlyn or her land. Her acreage crested the rise of the ridge, giving Kendrick Ridge its vantage point and its name. Her land abutted his and linked his to two other neighbors. Phase One of the project would only go ahead with that middle parcel: Devlyn's land.

That meant seeing her tomorrow. Rye never took the easy way first. The other property owners were already interested in selling. He knew that.

Dev would be different because his deal came packed with a whole lot of painful history.

He took the turn onto Route 321 and headed for B&B Cabins. A small town like Kendrick Creek didn't offer hotel and motel lodging, but a smattering of cabin rentals had sprung up over the years. As long as it had a decent bed and Wi-Fi, he was good to go.

He wanted to settle in and plan how he was going to approach Devlyn the next day. One way or another this project would move forward. Hopefully with Devlyn's land, but if he had to go to Plan B, he would. It wouldn't be as pretty. Devlyn's ridge allowed a magnificent view of the mountains east of the valley, and the lower land that bordered the northern edge of Rye's farmland was thickly forested. The wooded land changed the dynamics of the homesites. Either way, he'd be here for several weeks to put a plan in motion.

He turned into the broad driveway for B&B Cabins and parked outside the manager's small house, while a cat happily crunched on some kind of treat nearby.

His key was taped to the door in an envelope. "Had an errand. Make yourself at home. Cabin five. We'll finish stuff up tomorrow. B. Taylor."

God bless the small-town mentality that trusted he wouldn't take advantage of the older lady who'd taken his reservation the day before.

He took the key, got back in his car and drove up the curving drive to cabin five. The yard was well lit with dusk-to-dawn lights. The cabin was typical: rustic and simple. A door was centered between two identical windows. Colorful pansies broke up the wood-on-wood of the small porch, wood railings and wooden steps, while different-colored tulips bobbed their heads in narrow rectangular plots in front of the porch.

He opened the cabin door before hauling things in from the trunk of his car. The souped-up sports car had been his reward for his first major financial success years ago. He had just taken it out of storage this week, another sign of the changing seasons.

He grabbed sheets and blankets and carried them inside to the small bedroom. He could honestly say he'd never stayed in a place where he had to provide his own linens before. Clearly there was a first time for everything.

He went back for his laptop case and suitcases as a small car rolled up the driveway. It drove by him and pulled into one of the two parking spots in front of the cabin next door.

He carried a suitcase in, set it down and headed back outside.

He glanced to the right.

And his heart stopped.

Devlyn.

Ten years fell away in a heartbeat. She still wore her hair long. Long, curly blond hair that had a mind of its own. Beautiful profile.

She looked up at the same moment.

Their eyes met.

Hers went wide with shock and then something else. Something that looked too much like fear to be anything else.

Her attention shifted away briefly.

A boy raced out. "I'll get that stuff, Mom. No worries! And thanks for helping me with my geography homework. I'm glad that's done!"

The boy grabbed a couple of bags from the back seat of a well-used car and hustled them into the house. A boy who looked like Devlyn but had a cowlick over his forehead, a swirl of wayward hair. The same cowlick that Rye saw in the mirror every single day of his life.

He stared at the boy. A boy about nine years old or so.

Then he lifted his gaze to Devlyn, and the look on her face told Rye everything he needed to know.

He had a child.

A boy.

And she'd kept him a secret all these years.

His heart crashed.

His hands went numb. A coil of anger snaked its way up his spine, an anger so raw and powerful that he couldn't define it, much less contain it.

He had a son. A boy he knew nothing about. A boy whose worn clothing and scuffed shoes illustrated the kind of life Rye had escaped over thirty years before.

Did she hate him so much that she deliberately kept the boy from him?

He couldn't think and didn't dare react. Not yet. Not when his brain was on fire. He'd schooled himself on the art of negotiation over the years. Going in hot generally meant coming out cold and empty-handed, so he took a breath. A deep one. And watched the emotions play out on her face.

God, help me.

The silent prayer was no help as Devlyn realized that ten years of silence had just come to a screeching halt.

Rye looked at her.

She looked back.

Her throat convulsed, not from tears.

Devlyn had steeled herself against tears over Rye Bauer a long time ago, but this wasn't how she'd seen this happening. She had, in fact, never seen it happening, especially since his grandparents' farm had stood vacant the past few years, before the wildfire wiped out multiple properties on Kendrick Mills Road.

Rye. Here. Now.

And Jed, her beautiful son, suddenly thrust into a mess created years ago when Rye walked away from her without a backward glance.

The years had been kind to him. His light brown hair was cut short and barely tinged with gray. Laugh lines framed the brown eyes she remembered so well. Too well.

Sharp clothes. A fancy car. The sunglasses he had propped on his head probably cost more than the annual clothing budget for her and Jed combined.

She tried to swallow.

She couldn't. The lump in her throat

was too thick. She became instantly aware of her shabby shoes, the aged car, the hand-me-downs Jed wore, gifts from other Kendrick Creek families.

She wanted to sprint to the cabin door and close it before he saw Jed, but Jed raced her way right then, grinning. A wonderful boy, the love and light of her life these past ten years.

Jed was talking to her.

She couldn't make sense of his words.

Not with Rye staring at him like that.

She knew the moment realization dawned. His gaze lifted from Jed to her with a look of such hurt that she should have been ashamed.

She wasn't.

She wasn't the one who'd walked away.

She hadn't given him the cold shoulder and moved on with her life.

He had.

He'd made his choices.

Then she'd made hers.

But seeing him here brought crushing guilt, and she'd had enough of that when her mother was alive, thank you very much. She hadn't needed it then and she refused to embrace it now.

Actions had consequences.

Rye callously cut her loose a decade before. Whatever he was doing in Kendrick Creek had nothing to do with her. She'd see to that.

She took the last bag of groceries from the car and followed Jed inside.

Then she closed and locked the cabin door.

She had nowhere to run. Nowhere to hide.

She didn't sleep that night, but Devlyn had been a single mom for a long time. This wasn't her first sleepless night. But this one wasn't caused by worry or illness.

It was caused by Rye Bauer, the man she'd loved, showing up in Kendrick Creek out of the blue.

Why was he here?

Land.

Rye had been a real estate developer for years. The destructive fire that had raced across their valley three months ago had created a wealth of opportunities for investors.

A lot of folks had lost everything, and when some folks lost, others stood to gain. Rye was clearly one of the others.

Her heart was shaken. Her gut had clenched when their eyes met and hadn't relaxed yet. How could it? Ten years of living a lie had finally caught up to her.

She looked bad the next morning. No sleep and ugly crying was a tough combination at forty-four years old, but this wasn't about her. It was about Jed.

She asked Biddy Taylor to make sure Jed got on the school bus, and as soon as the bus lights faded up the road, she crossed the gravel, climbed the steps and rapped on his door.

A part of her hoped he wouldn't answer.

But a glimmer of strength soared within

her because she'd been keeping her son safe and sound for a decade. Nothing and no one was going to sully that track record now.

The door opened.

Rye stood there.

Anger she would have denied feeling roared to life, and going by his expression, his fury surpassed hers.

He folded his arms. "It seems we have something to discuss, Devlyn."

"We do." Her heart pounded in her chest, but she faced him, wishing he didn't look so put together when she felt torn apart. "You need to leave Kendrick Creek. Whatever you're doing here, it has nothing to do with us, and I won't have you messing up our lives. You may have money and clout in Knoxville, but no one and nothing is going to mess up my son's life. Especially not you."

"*Our* son."

The words cut her like a hot knife on butter.

"The son you kept hidden from me."

She rolled her eyes. "Hidden in plain sight. If you had ever bothered to come to town, to come home, even to visit your grandmother or close up her house when she moved to Knoxville. We weren't hidden, Rye. We were right here, all the while. You just never bothered to check."

Her words hit him hard. She saw that and didn't care.

She'd been naive in her twenties and fairly gullible in her thirties, but now she wasn't anyone's fool. Dealing with Rye and living with her mother's constant disapproval had toughened her.

"The bottom line is that you never bothered to tell me," he shot back. "Why, Dev?"

He'd always called her Dev, but back then the name was laced with warmth and love.

Not anymore.

"You could have called me," he continued. "Emailed me. Sent me a birth notice. 'Hey, it's a boy!'" He made a face of intentional surprise. "'And by the way—he's yours!'"

He sounded bitter.

Well, too bad, but even as that thought crossed her mind, she realized he had every right to be bitter. She'd had her turn. Now it was his, it seemed.

"What's his name?"

"Jed."

"After your dad."

She drew a deep breath and seared him with a look. "Yes, and that's the only thing you need to know, Rye. You didn't want me back then, and we don't need you now, so I'm sorry you stumbled on us here—"

"You lost your house in the fire."

He knew that? He must have been checking out fire reports online overnight. She hated that he knew her troubles, but she shrugged it off as if it wasn't a big deal. "It was just a house. Jed and I got out alive. Nothing else matters."

"And no insurance of record at the town offices, but also no mortgage, so it wouldn't necessarily be registered. Did you have homeowner's insurance, Dev?"

She'd let the policy lapse nearly three years ago, when her mother had died and left her money in a trust for Jed. Devlyn had inherited the house, and all the bills that went along with it, but the money was inaccessible, even for necessities. Her mother had seen to that with the help of a local attorney.

Molly McCabe had loved Jed, but she'd hated that her daughter had brought shame to the family with an out-of-wedlock child. In her own quiet way she'd never let Devlyn forget it. The bequest to Jed, with no reference to Devlyn, simply underscored her disappointment in a miscreant daughter. "This is none of your business, Rye. None," she repeated firmly. The chill of the morning rolled down the mountain in a blanket of cold air. She fought a shiver. "Go somewhere else. Stay somewhere else. There is no reason for you to be here, in the cabin next door to us."

He leaned against the door frame and held her gaze. "There are two very good reasons, Devlyn."

He'd gone to her full name.

Good. He had no right to small amenities of familiarity.

"The first is my son."

She huffed out a breath, and it puffed a cloud of steam into the air. Air that would warm quickly once the sun crested the mountain. Rye went on before she could respond.

"The second is your land. My development company is presenting a proposal to the town for an adult living community on Kendrick Mills Road and your land is right in the middle of it. You're why I'm here. You're why I came to town. But that beautiful boy you called Jed?" He jutted his chin toward the school bus stop down by the roadside. "He's the reason I'll be staying as long as I need to. I lived a life without a father, and now that I know I have a son, I'm going to do everything in my power to make sure he knows he's got a father who'll be there for him through thick and thin. Now that I know he exists, of course."

He wanted her land.

And her son.

She thought she'd be able to handle this face-to-face without getting angry. She was older. More mature. But the injustice that Rye had swept into town and might be holding all the cards when it came to her child and her financial stability was too much.

She stared at him—right at him—and didn't back down. Wouldn't back down. Not when there was so much at stake. "You won't get my son and you won't get my land, so you might as well pack up and go home because there is nothing for you here. And there never will be."

She turned and walked away.

He would have lawyers.

She didn't.

He had money.

She was flat broke.

But she had something he didn't.

Faith.

And right now the beautiful verse from Joshua rang through her mind, the verse that commanded her to be strong and of great courage.

She'd cling to that verse because Rye might have come here to change the face of Kendrick Creek, but she held two elements of that proposal.

Her land.

And her son.

And Rye Bauer wasn't about to get his hands on either.

Chapter Two

Devlyn was angry.

Well, join the club, Rye thought as he closed the door to his cabin with a firm smack.

Warring emotions raced through him.

He'd been up most of the night since she parked her car, wondering how this had happened, but he knew how. He'd stayed away from Kendrick Creek, away from his grandmother, away from their sprawling farm because he'd been deliberately avoiding Devlyn. They'd been childhood neighbors. Then they met again as adults, both working in Knoxville. They'd fallen in love, but he'd walked away. She'd moved back here after their breakup. He'd even gone the extra measure and had brought Grandmaw to Knoxville when her health began to fail.

You could have checked on Devlyn.

The accuracy of the scolding hurt. He'd professed love for her, but had never followed up, partly because he didn't want to see her go on with a life that didn't include him. Was that integrity or cowardice?

It was both and that shamed him, but nothing he'd done made her choice all right.

Easy for you to say. You weren't the one that got dumped.

He took a breath, said a prayer for patience and drove to Kendrick Mills Road to get a firsthand look at the land.

Reality gut-punched him again when his grandparents' farm came into view.

He'd hired a crew to do demolition on

the burned-out structures, but nothing could have prepared him for the raw visual of their empty homesite and the one lone barn that somehow had escaped the fire's wrath.

The targeted area for the development project lay just shy of the county line and west of the fire-damaged part of town. Thirty-two acres of his family's farm would be incorporated into the plan. On the south side, Devlyn's thirteen-acre parcel sat higher, offering scenic views from the upper road leading into the proposed community. Procuring her land was crucial to his plans. He needed to make this work. But how?

Just then, his phone rang. Roseanne Bindler's number showed up. Roseanne had been his friend and now his partner in Smoky Mountain Development. He took the call as he walked up the road he'd traveled many times as a boy. "Good morning, Rose. I'm walking up Kendrick Mills Road right now, and let me tell you, it's a kick in the head to see what happened here. But it's also a glimpse of the future. Or what the future could be," he amended. "Let me show you what I'm seeing." He switched to video and scanned the area in a gentle arc. He named the parcels as they came into view, and when he got to Devlyn's, Roseanne whistled in appreciation, even though Devlyn's house lot was still a mess.

"That place is key, Rye. The perfect vantage point for the upper road arc you planned."

"I know." Rye wished it weren't the case. The slope of Devlyn's acreage offered prime homesites. "But if it doesn't work out, we've got Plan B." He turned the phone's camera downslope where Miles Conrad's land met the road. The lower forested land changed the dynamic of the concept. It was still nice, but it didn't have the majesty of the original plan. Conrad's land would offer wooded privacy and some owners would like that, but it removed the hillside angle that Devlyn's land ensured, and that was key to the beauty of the development. "But the original plan is definitely our priority right now."

"Without a doubt. But, wow." She breathed softly. "That fire did a number on this area." Roseanne's voice deepened with compassion as Rye zoomed into his grandparents' site. "That was where you grew up? Where you and your mom lived?"

"Yeah."

"I'm so sorry, Rye."

"Me, too." He hadn't expected to be moved by the stark emptiness of Grandmaw and Granddad's land. He'd seen pictures from the demo and cleanup crew. He knew it was gone. But the reality still hit hard.

Seeing it in person didn't just hurt. It crushed his heart, and he'd have thought himself invincible.

Wrong.

All he could envision were Grandmaw's pictures, cluttering every wall in the house. The blankets she'd made, the quilts she'd created. Her handiwork gone forever.

If he'd ever bothered to come home, he could have put some things in storage, but he hadn't done that. He'd stayed away and lost the opportunity. An opportunity that seemed to matter more now that he knew he had a son.

"You all right?"

He breathed deep and shrugged one shoulder. "Yeah. Just a little numb. I knew what I was going to encounter, but it's still a shock. My brain keeps trying to put things back into place."

"You okay with us moving ahead, Rye?"

Roseanne wasn't just a good person. She was a great one, all heart. "Yeah. Grandmaw would approve of our idea. She always said hang on to the land…

but it doesn't have to be the same land. She believed that real estate was money in the bank."

"Wise woman."

She was. Her wisdom had inspired him to go into real estate and development, and he'd kept her close to him and his mother her final few years.

But now he wished he'd given thought to the history of his family, this farm, the old house, while it stood there. The empty site mocked him. "I'll call you later, all right?"

"Right."

He disconnected the call as he approached the McCabe property.

Like Grandmaw's, it had been destroyed, along with two other properties on this road. That made the fire a rough toll for a small community, but Devlyn's homestead hadn't been cleared yet. The ugliness of the fire-ravaged home was another wake-up call.

His son had been in that house as it burned. And she'd gotten him out.

That was something to thank God for.

As he approached the McCabe driveway, a familiar small gray car came over the rise from the other direction, and there was no mistaking the animosity in Devlyn's eyes when she saw him in her driveway. But she didn't run him over, so he counted that as a victory.

She pulled in, parked the car and hopped out. "What are you doing here?"

He splayed his hands. "My job. I wanted to see what this looked like up close, and I only have one thing to say, Dev." He turned and scanned his grandparents' site and hers. "I'm so sorry."

His sincerity made her pause, but not for long.

"We're all sorry, Rye. The scope of that fire didn't just affect the people whose homes were ruined, or the businesses that went up in flames. The ripple effect messes up everyone in a small town like this. When jobs and businesses go under, that's a huge deal. Even people who kept their house or their mobile home are feeling aftereffects from the destruction. How convenient of you to show up three months later, waving a checkbook to tempt people to sell."

"That's unfair."

"Is it?" She folded her arms and raised her eyebrows. "Never let a good crisis go to waste."

"That's not what brought me here, Devlyn." He met her gaze straight on. "I developed this plan last fall, before the holidays." When she looked doubtful, he pointed up the road. "Ask the Smiths and the Costellos. I approached them about using a portion of their properties to round out the acreage I needed for the development. That's why your property is in the middle. I hadn't approached you yet because I knew our history would make this difficult."

"Because you dumped me, you mean?"

She was right, and he'd done it because he'd needed a firm break. Only the reason he'd walked away hadn't occurred. Despite his fears, he was amazingly healthy and looked foolish right now. "Yes. But be fair. I didn't know you were pregnant, Dev."

Her expression changed. She looked almost sad, but not for her. For him. "That wouldn't have changed anything, Rye. I am not desperate for anyone's attention. A woman wants to be loved for herself, not because she's carrying someone's child. If you didn't want me, there was really nothing more to say. No doubt you moved on fairly quickly."

He hadn't. Oh, he'd tried. He'd dated. He'd had a couple of almost-serious relationships, but he'd held back for the same reason he'd walked away from the beautiful woman standing in front of him. If he was going to inherit his father's midlife illness, he'd do it alone. Only at forty-seven years old, it hadn't happened.

He was hale, hearty and healthy, and that made his worry seem downright foolish.

He let the conversation drop. It wasn't the time or the place to get into old news. Not when he had an important agenda.

Clouds drifted in and the wind turned chilly. Devlyn snugged her jacket more firmly around her middle. She moved forward.

"What are you doing?"

"I need to see if anything's survived. Mementos. Stuff buried under the wood. Bobby Ray Carlson has offered to do demo for me."

He remembered the big, burly football player. He'd been a year behind Rye and two years ahead of Devlyn in high school. Funny, Rye had been Devlyn's neighbor for years as children, and they barely knew each other back then. She'd been a pesky little kid, and he'd liked working the farm with his granddad. "You're going into the house?"

"I don't know any other way to check

things out. I can't do it with Jed around, and I've been babysitting two little girls for the Trembeths. I have today free and the weather's calmed down. Although the top of this hill likes to catch the wind."

He'd forgotten that, but she was right. Grandmaw's farm was recessed enough to stay sheltered some of the time, but the wind blew free up here. "What are you looking for?"

"Pictures. Anything that might make a difference to Jed as he grows up. I have some current pictures on my phone, but nothing of his grandparents. How my dad would drive him around in that old red pickup, searching out the best Christmas tree. Or how my mom would take him into town for a haircut because a fine young man deserved fine hair."

"They loved him."

He saw the subtle change in her expression before she masked it. "Very much."

"I'm glad of that." Rye pulled the zipper up on his jacket and moved forward with her. "Let's check things out."

"No."

She looked horrified by the thought of him accompanying her, but Rye wasn't about to let her traipse into the skeleton of a house on her own. "You're not doing this alone. What if a timber falls on you?"

"It won't. The fire chief was here and said the walls were solid."

"That means we both get to live. Good deal." He moved forward. She hurried to catch up.

"Listen, Rye—"

He kept moving.

"I know you think you're being nice, but trust me," she continued as he strode toward the burned-out structure, "being here with you makes me homicidal, so you might want to reconsider your actions."

That almost made him smile. "I don't

think you'd actually kill me, Dev. Although the day ain't over."

"Rye—"

"After you." He'd moved up the steps and pulled open the listing door. The steps were solid enough, but half the porch was missing. If he had a brain, he'd have insisted they not do this, but if the house was slated for demo, he understood her need to see what she might find in the rubble.

He hadn't taken time to preserve anything of his grandparents' place, so his son would have few mementos of them, but he could help scour for things from the boy's other grandparents. He held the door while she stepped in.

Disaster awaited them inside. Between the ravages of fire, smoke and water, the place was a wreck. The dank stench reeked of burned, wet wood and something else. Something awful. As they neared the kitchen, he realized it was the refrigerator and freezer.

"Oh, that's dreadful."

Dev put a hand over her face, but then she spied something on what was left of an inner wall. A set of pictures had survived the onslaught and she drew them off the wall with eager hands. They were damaged, but not badly, and there was no mistaking her joy with this surprising discovery.

Her parents' wedding picture. A picture of her and her brother Tommy. Tommy had been killed in Desert Storm. She'd worn one of those rubber bracelet things while they were dating, one that commemorated Tommy, and he wondered if she still wore it. Had she eventually taken it off?

A picture of Tommy in uniform. It had been water damaged, but looked salvageable. And a picture of her and Jed, standing by the old tree that held a swing out back. A swing he'd used as a kid when he hung out with Tommy, one she'd used when they'd go off on teen missions and leave the pesky little sister behind.

She clutched the pictures tightly. "If there's nothing else at all, these are enough of a blessing because I didn't think I'd find anything."

Rye checked around the room. He used the flashlight on his cell phone. He had a higher-powered one in the car, but didn't need to retrieve it. Everything that had been on a horizontal surface was ruined. "I think these survived because they were on that inside wall."

"Just enough protection to preserve them."

The fire damage was extensive, but that one section of wall had suffered only minor scorch marks and nothing more.

Something creaked overhead. Enough to make Rye take Devlyn's arm. "The wind is picking up, Dev. Let's not tempt fate."

For just a moment, she looked at him like she used to, the look of trust and love that he'd cherished, but it was gone in a flash.

She pulled her arm loose and moved ahead. When she got to the door, she paused and looked back. Her eyes roamed the ruins.

Was she remembering good times?

Was she lamenting loss?

He didn't know, and her silence told him nothing, but seeing her expression made him realize something. He'd give anything to wipe that look away. That was a sobering thought because he hadn't come here to renew a relationship he'd deliberately ruined.

He was here to acquire her land. And his actions weren't going to wipe away the angst on her face. They were guaranteed to make it worse.

Chapter Three

Devlyn let her eyes roam the wrecked interior of her parents' home one last time.

She'd experienced a lot of joy growing up here. The sorrow had come later when her mother's grief over losing her husband had turned to anger at her daughter's situation.

Molly McCabe had loved Jed, but she'd been bitterly disappointed in Devlyn, and that had overshadowed the final years of her mother's life. She'd needed Devlyn as her mobility issues worsened, and maybe that sparked more anger because her mother didn't like being dependent.

She was gone now, but she'd tied up her money in a trust for Jed, leaving Devlyn to struggle. Worse, she'd done it deliberately, as punishment.

Devlyn pushed away from the door and moved down the steps.

Rye closed the door behind her.

She wasn't sure why he'd done that.

Bobby Ray would come by with his demo crew and sweep the lot clean. She'd begin again, with nothing this time. Nothing but the work of her hands and her son.

Rye caught up to her. "We need to talk."

"Not now."

He didn't stop. "We're both here. Or we could go grab coffee somewhere. Or food. I'm pretty sure you didn't eat this morning. I know I didn't. Let me at least show you my proposal, Dev."

"Not interested." She kept moving toward her car, but his next words stopped her in her tracks.

"Seventy-five thousand dollars."

She swung back his way. "Nothing here goes for that kind of price."

"Your land connects both sides of the hill. It's key, so yes. It's worth every penny of that offer."

She swallowed hard.

He didn't pressure her, and that almost made her not want to hit him for holding the advantage in what felt like a very unfair deal.

Not unfair because of the price. That was far more than she would have anticipated.

But unfair because the last person she wanted to throw her a lifeline was the man standing there, with an open escape route out of poverty.

The wind kicked up again, fiercer this time.

"If you don't want to grab food or coffee, we can go back to the cabins and I'll show you the proposal. It incorporates land from all four properties. Yours. Mine. Smith's and Costello's."

She didn't want to listen to him. She didn't want his money to become her saving grace, but the facts were simple. Someone needed to buy this property. She had no money to rebuild. The land was her sole piece of equity, and his offer was generous.

He dumped you without a hint of emotion and you know he's going to stir up trouble for you and Jed. Remember the story about the never-satisfied mouse? Once you start something, it's real hard to stop it.

Rye hadn't gotten his fancy car and sharp-looking clothes by handing away money. No doubt he could bankroll a legal team in a custody battle.

She couldn't.

Her mind went numb. Trying to sort the business from the personal loomed impossible because they intertwined.

She took a deep breath and opened her car door. "I don't want to talk about this now."

He waited, quiet.

"This whole thing, the fire, the house, you being here." She drew her brows down. "It's like Murphy's Law cubed."

"Everything that can go wrong will, and at the worst possible time. But maybe this isn't things going wrong." He stayed where he was, but his expression showed concern. "Maybe it's the beginning of things going right."

She sent him a look of disbelief. "Forgive me if I say that you rank low on my list of people to trust. Why would I put my future in the hands of someone who treated me so poorly ten years ago? So I can be made a fool twice?"

"There's nothing shady about the offer, Dev."

She wasn't about to fall into that trap. "So you say. Send it over. I'll have my people go over it."

He accepted that with a look of compassion, but he wanted her land, so of course he'd act compassionate. Up until the contract was signed. Then it would be gloves off.

"I'll drop a hard copy at your cabin and email you a copy. That way you can share it with your people as needed."

He didn't scoff at the thought of her having people.

She deliberately hadn't said her lawyer because she couldn't afford a lawyer, but Shane Stone was rebuilding a good portion of the town and he'd know the ins and outs of land contracts. He dealt with them all the time. And Doc Mary and Jess Bristol were doctors. They were educated women who would keep her from making a major mistake. "All right." She settled the pictures into the back seat of the car and climbed into the driver's side. She didn't wave to him or even acknowledge him as she backed out of the driveway.

Should she play nice with him? Would that help or hinder whatever might happen with Jed?

She understood the Biblical verse where King Solomon offered to cut a child in half to appease two women, both of whom claimed to be the child's mother. The real mother relinquished her claim immediately to spare her child's life.

And it wasn't even that she hated the thought of Jed meeting his father. The boy deserved that.

It was the result that scared her.

Would Jed hate her for never telling him about Rye? For keeping him hidden? When he'd asked about his father in the past, she'd always brushed it off, letting him know that it was just the two of them, and that was okay.

Now she'd have to admit that she'd been lying.

She'd kept the truth from her son. How was a boy supposed to forgive that? He wasn't old enough to understand the complexities of a relationship and how gut-punched she'd been when Rye had tossed her over.

She'd been seeing picket fences and front porch swings, while Rye had gone off to greener pastures. Judging from his upscale appearance, his dream came true.

Hers didn't. But she had Jed, and that had been a saving grace. But now—

She called Jess Bristol as she headed toward town. "I need girlfriend time, ASAP."

"I've got two patients waiting. Then I'm free for thirty minutes. Come on over. Coffee's on."

She stopped and bought ten dollars of gas on the way.

She eyed the candy bars, but didn't buy one, and it wasn't because of the cost.

It was because Rye Bauer was in town, and she wasn't about to let him or his agenda push her into gaining back the ten pounds she'd lost after the fire. She put the temptation to anxiety-eat on hold and drove to Kendrick Creek Medical's newly renovated office, where she spilled her guts to her good friend, expecting to feel better.

She didn't.

Rye set up appointments with the Smiths and the Costellos. Both sessions went smoothly. He had to increase both offers, but he'd anticipated that. When he'd finished those meetings, he headed back up Kendrick Mills Road. As he crested the ridge, the demolition crew was rolling into the McCabe driveway.

He looked for Devlyn's car.

It wasn't there.

He couldn't blame her. Watching your childhood home be demolished would be tough. And just as he was thinking that, another thought came to him.

The swing.

It wasn't fancy, and it might be damaged, but that tree swing had been Devlyn's escape when they were youngsters.

He turned into the driveway behind the excavator and shovel, only he pulled around the back of the house.

Then he frowned in realization.

Cool sports cars didn't work on wet, slick Tennessee soil, and they sure didn't accommodate a two-person wooden swing.

He ran his fingers through his hair as someone approached from the other side of the house. "Hey, bud, you can't be back here. Sorry."

He turned.

Bobby Ray was headed his way. He looked older, but still built like a linebacker. He stuck out a hand in greeting. "Bobby Ray, it's Rye Bauer. Bauer Farm." He jutted his chin north. "I saw you guys pulling in and I want to save the swing there."

"In that?" Bobby Ray lifted an amused eyebrow as he indicated Rye's ride. "Rye, there ain't no way that swing is going in that car."

"I see that," said Rye, bemused.

"I'll tell you what. My brother Ed is here with his pickup. How about we take the swing down and he drops it over on your land next door? Because Devlyn doesn't exactly have a place to store it, you know?"

He knew, all right. The swing was singed, and one side of the heavy rope had broken, but it was salvageable. "I'll get it fixed up for her and get it back to her once she's settled."

Bobby Ray appraised him for a moment, then agreed. "Sounds like a plan, as long as it gets back to Devlyn and Jed. They've gone through enough these past few years. They didn't need this, but then, no one did. I'll see to it, Rye. And hey." Bobby Ray reached out a hand. "Welcome home."

"Thanks, man." He didn't bother to say that Kendrick Creek wasn't his home and hadn't been in over twenty-five years because maybe the place you grew up was home. Kind of. He had a life, a beautiful home, a thriving business and an excess of everyday choices back in Knoxville.

Kendrick Creek was nothing like Knoxville.

He got back in his car, managed to turn it around and drove north. When he headed toward town, he stopped at the Kendrick Creek Feed & Seed along the way. Miles Conrad was the co-owner of the big store, but he was also the owner of a parcel of Kendrick Mills Road land that was slated for Rye's alternate plan. If Devlyn refused to sell, that would affect the Smiths and the Costellos because his Plan B went north of Bauer Farm. Plan A went south, and that made Devlyn's decision extremely important to those two families.

He walked into the store. A middle-aged woman was at one of the two registers. She greeted him with a friendly smile. "'Morning, y'all. Welcome to the Feed & Seed."

The personal greeting was a nice touch. He smiled back at her. "I'm here to see Miles Conrad. If he's in?"

"Down aisle one, all the way to the back."

He followed the aisle as directed. The store was well stocked for the spring up-tick in business. It wasn't as busy as he'd expected in early April, when all of Eastern Tennessee was plowing, disking and planting.

As he approached the office, raised voices made him pause. He was about to leave and call Conrad for an appointment, but another middle-aged woman hurried out of the office just then, her eyes rimmed with red. A solidly built man exited the office after her.

"Miles Conrad?" He asked the question politely but didn't extend his hand because he wasn't a fan of making people cry.

"Who's asking?"

Hairs stood up along Rye's neck. He made note of that reaction and answered pleasantly. "Rye Bauer. Smoky Mountain Development."

Conrad's expression changed instantly, another red flag. People whose faces morphed that quickly had way too much practice at pretense, but he wasn't here to pass judgment on the man's character. He was here to clear a path for the land he needed to move this development forward, and that plan might include Conrad's parcel.

"Bauer! Good to meet you. The idea you folks sent me was a good one and this town needs some development. I've been saying that for a long time."

"It's a prime site with great potential." Rye kept his comment purposely neutral. "I'm looking at several options to see what would best serve our designs, and your property is a possibility."

Conrad's chest puffed out. "Prime land,

great road frontage, access to town and thirty minutes from all of the attractions in Gatlinburg, Pigeon Forge and Sevierville. You can't go wrong when so many things are going right."

"Mostly we're impressed with how quickly the town is moving to replace and repair buildings damaged by the fire."

Conrad's chest puffed up. "Folks don't hold back in Tennessee," he told Rye. Tennessee had a "let's fix it" mentality when it came to adversity or natural disasters. "I'm proud to see things coming back to life, and a good share of the repairs will be done before the tourist season hits high gear. That speaks highly of me and my community, Mr. Bauer."

"Call me Rye. Please." Rye indicated the Feed & Seed with a glance. "Nice store you've got here."

"It's been in my family for two generations," bragged Conrad.

Rye accepted that, even though he

knew for a fact that the store was co-owned by the Kendrick family. The information was on the public record, and the Kendricks actually held a majority, but there were no Kendricks living in Cocke County and only one in neighboring Sevier County. "Well, it's a great place."

"We've got everything the farmer, rancher and homeowner needs," Conrad went on. "Can I show you around?"

Rye declined politely. "I'm on my way to check a few things. Another time."

"Of course." Conrad followed him toward the door. "Glad to touch base with you. It's about time we changed things up to go with the times. It'll help our businesses, sure enough."

"Folks would be fortunate to live here, sir." Rye left the store, thoughtful.

The store owner had made a worker cry, then put on a happy face for Rye.

Rye found the actions disturbing.

His mother had worked service jobs all

her life, and she'd dealt with her share of disrespect and harassment. It wasn't something he allowed in his firm or the companies he did business with. But if he needed Conrad's land, he needed to toe the middle line, a skill he'd developed as a real estate investor.

He didn't have to like the person. He just had to seal the deal.

Chapter Four

He drove into the town and pulled into the church parking lot. He exited the car and took a deep breath.

Country air.

He'd forgotten how absolutely pristine it was.

He loved the city. Loved his job. He'd made a difference in a lot of good ways, but there was something pure about the air here. As if God Himself filtered out the bad stuff and only left the good.

Grandmaw had talked like that about the town and the farms surrounding it.

He hadn't listened. He'd left Kendrick Creek wanting bigger. Better. Brighter.

Now, crossing the parking lot, he wished he'd listened more. He emerged just south of the old hardware store and took in the town's progress.

The hardware store stood empty, but clean windows and fresh paint had brought the big square building back to life.

Across the road, a woman was painting the outside of an old home. The fresh coat of yellow paint reflected the sun's rays. New construction was nearly complete on two buildings facing him. Buildings that had been completely destroyed by the fire were in the final stages of being rebuilt. That was a big selling point for prospective buyers in the proposed subdivision.

An old man was strolling up the road. A big black-and-tan German shepherd walked in step with the elderly man, not pulling. Not leading. Just walking along, a picture-perfect pairing.

They strolled past a new building marked Kendrick Creek Medical, and along that whole side of the road was the framework for a sidewalk.

Sidewalks?

In Kendrick Creek?

The thought made him smile, but it disappeared when he saw Devlyn come out of the medical office.

His heart went quiet, too, which seemed ridiculous because there were really no excuses for what she'd done. Not good ones. She'd kept the boy from him out of spite. How was he supposed to forgive that?

And you lied about why you walked away.

Why was she at the medical office?

Was she ill?

The thought that she could be clenched his gut. Bobby Ray had just said that Devlyn and Jed had been through enough. Were things worse than he knew?

The urge to help her and Jed swept over him.

Just then, Devlyn drove his way.

She spotted him.

A flash of worry deepened her features, but then she looked straight ahead and drove by.

She didn't know what to make of this whole thing. Neither did he, but they were next-door neighbors for at least a few weeks, and he'd make that time count. For him. For her. And for their son.

He grabbed a sandwich at a convenience store up the road, and when he drove back to the cabins, an older woman hailed him just inside the entrance. He pulled into one of the three parking spaces in front of the tiny house bordering the road and climbed out. "Mrs. Taylor?"

"Biddy'll do." She jerked her head in

a crisp fashion toward the door. "I was called to a sickbed last night, so I couldn't greet you proper. Sorry about that."

"No problem. Your instructions were clear."

"One thing they can say about me," she told him with a wry smile. "I'm clear as a summer day. Sometimes too direct, but I take that as a compliment."

"I like straight talk myself," he told her.

She lifted both brows while still looking down at the cabin registry. "Can't say that about most salesmen."

"Maybe real estate buyers are different."

She snorted. "As if. But the jury's out on you, young man."

Rye couldn't remember the last time he was called a young man. It felt good, and that made him feel old. But forty-seven wasn't old.

It was seasoned.

"You handy?"

He frowned. "I'm not sure what you mean."

"Around a place. With a hammer and a drill. You know. Useful."

"I can hold my own."

"My Ray died a year back."

"I'm sorry."

She looked up as if to see if he meant it, then grimaced. "I am, too. He wasn't overly handy himself, but between us we got things done. This year I've got a few chores that need tending and my shoulders hit a flare."

He frowned.

"The arthritis. It's bad and the pills don't seem to help much. The damp, most likely."

"The cold, wet weather bothers your joints."

"Isn't that what I said?"

Kind of. He began again. "Mrs. Taylor—"

"Everyone calls me Biddy. It's my name. Not an insult."

That made him smile. "I'd be glad to help. I don't know how much time I'll have, but I can give you a hand or two."

"Now, that's the talk." Her smile showed approval. She was missing a tooth on the lower left side, but that didn't change the sweetness of her smile. "If you've got time tomorrow, I've got some wood that needs replacing on two of the cabins. We were blessed to escape fire damage, but these old buildings are showing their age and they need to be kept up. Folks don't care about fancy, but they do care about nice, don't they?"

"I expect they do."

"I'll fix your rent depending on how much help you can do."

"No, ma'am, you will not," he said firmly. "I'll pay my cabin fees like any guest, and I'll help you because my mama raised me right."

Her smile widened. "I didn't know your mama, Rye Bauer, but I knew your grandmaw Marge. We sewed some together before she left town. Quilting and knitting, depending on the day and season and whatever mood struck us. She was a good woman, and the things she made brought a pretty price at that little co-op Devlyn had in the front of the McCabe place. And Devlyn always gave Marge's things a great display spot. Marge Bauer sold a lot of stuff off o' that old front porch, let me tell you. She was a clever one, that Marge."

Grandmaw had been part of a sewing group?

A cooperative?

That was news to Rye.

She'd never mentioned the group or that she missed it. She'd seemed perfectly content to move into a senior living apartment in Knoxville. Biddy's words made him wonder if Grandmaw had only pretended satisfaction. It would have fit her giving nature. "She sure was."

Looking west, Biddy scanned the sky.

"It looks clear and a bit warmer tomorrow, so I'll see you then, if that suits. Whatever time works for you."

"You can read the weather from the sky?"

She withdrew a smartphone from her pocket. "This, mostly."

He grinned. He didn't have any meetings set up for the morning, so he made an appointment in his calendar on his smartphone. "Nine o'clock. All right?"

"Nine's good." She was making notes as he left. He got into the car, pulled around the drive and parked outside his cabin.

Devlyn's car wasn't parked next door. But around eight that evening he heard it pull in. The next morning, he watched as Jed made his way down the curving drive to catch the school bus just shy of eight o'clock.

Devlyn pulled out soon after.

Where did she go? What did she do?

He didn't know, but he put on the serviceable clothes he kept packed for scouting real estate ventures and showed up at Biddy's door just before nine.

She shot his attire a look of approval. "Prepared, I see."

"I've had to survey my share of property lines and unfinished construction," he told her. "One suitcase for meetings. One for the earthier side of my job."

She laughed softly as Devlyn pulled back into the driveway. She didn't look his way, but she noticed him and Biddy. He could tell by the way she lifted her chin and kept her gaze trained straight ahead.

Yeah. She noticed him, all right.

She pulled up to her cabin as he and Biddy removed a ladder off the backside of a service shed.

It was one of those old, lightweight aluminum ladders. Not rickety, but nothing to brag on, either.

They set it up along the side of cabin four, and he spotted the problem immediately. "It's not the flashing that's bad," he told her, and he hated to say it. Replacing the metal trim would have been a much cheaper fix. "This roof's gone sour underneath," he explained from his perch on the ladder. He used a putty knife to pry up the edge of the shingles.

She didn't look surprised. "We bought the place a dozen years back, and all of the cabins had new roofing installed, but we didn't realize they went over bad roofing. We've replaced all but two, but I figure my window of time is up on those two."

"If you want to prevent more water damage, mold and mildew, I agree. It's not cheap, though."

"I know the truth in that, but sometimes a body's got to draw on what they have to keep things going." She sounded stalwart but Rye read the truth in her eyes. The cost was a major worry when fire damage to the area might cut tourism over the next seven months. "I'll give the roofers a call."

"In the meantime, I can get this part started on my own. Are there dumpsters for hire for the roofing job?"

"There are. The guys will see to that."

Devlyn emerged from her cabin just then, two little girls skipping by her side. They were dressed in matching outfits, covered with some kind of spring flower print. Their little shirts sported hoods and they looked like a spring ad for a department store.

"A wadder!" The older girl shrieked in glee when she spotted the ladder up against the cabin. "I fink I wuv wadders so much, Miss Devwin!"

The littler girl frowned at the ladder, spotted him and burst into tears.

"Devlyn, come on over here. I've got something I wanted to say to you," called

Biddy. Dev came their way. She held tight to the littlest girl's hand, but the older girl skipped along as if she hadn't a care in the world.

"Hey, mister, you're up on a reawwy big wadder!" She parked her hands on tiny hips and tipped her head up to him with a look of astonishment. "You be vewy, vewy careful up there, you hear?"

"Can do, ma'am." He winked at the girl. Bless her heart, she burst out laughing as if he were the funniest man alive.

He wasn't. Not even close, but something about her joy made him more joyful. He shifted his gaze to Devlyn, but she stayed deliberately focused on Biddy. "Is there a problem here, Biddy?"

Biddy nodded. "Bad roofs on units two and four, and my fault for not getting to them before now."

"You've had a lot on your plate the past couple of years." Dev's comforting tone soothed the old woman's brow. "A body can only do so much, Biddy. You know that. And hospital bills take their share."

"I'll figure it out," Biddy replied. "I always do. God's watching over me and this place, and I've got a bit put by. But that's not what I wanted to talk to you about. I know you've got the girls today, but my sewing machine is just gathering dust these days, so I'm going to send it up to you. That way on the days when you're not minding Izzie and Beth you can work on things in your cabin."

Rye didn't miss the quick look of appreciation in Devlyn's eyes. He was pretty sure Biddy saw it, too.

"Except that *you* need it," Devlyn began, but Biddy shushed her quickly.

"If I did, which I don't, I wouldn't be offering," she stated plainly. "I've got notions that need to be used, too, a thread board that holds fifty spools and all sorts of things. No sense you not working while we're waiting for your store and work area to be finished, is there?"

"You're going to have a store, Dev?" Rye directed the question directly to her, and she looked up.

Absolutely lovely.

She was beautiful, and when those blue eyes met his, a shot of electricity went through him. He had to work hard to keep his face from showing his reaction, and he only managed to do it because keeping a straight face was essential in real estate negotiations. But it wasn't easy.

"Doc Mary is renting me one of her new buildings. When it's finished."

He frowned. "But what kind of store? What sort of stuff?"

"Like what me and your grandmaw did before she left," explained Biddy. "We worked together making stuff for Devlyn. She ran a store out of her house till the fire swept through. There's a whole bunch of us that make handmade things for her to sell. House things. Fabric. Wood. Metal. Stuff folks buy when they're coming through."

He heard what Biddy said, but he focused in on the crux of the matter. "You lost your home *and* your business?" He hadn't thought this could get worse.

It just did.

And when she nailed him with a steely gaze, he realized she wasn't looking for sympathy, especially not from him.

"Things can be replaced." She said it softly. Firmly. "Lives can't." She redirected her attention to Biddy. "I'm taking the girls up to Doc's place for the day, Biddy. Jed will get dropped off there. Then Hassie's grandniece is taking the girls for the next couple of weeks to give me time to work. Having your machine would be great. That will give me time to sew."

Biddy accepted the reply with a firm nod and Devlyn smiled. It was the first genuine smile he'd seen on her. He liked it. It felt good to see her happy. Then the image of Jed flooded back, a boy he'd been denied, and that pretty much negated his momentary altruism.

The older little girl drew attention back to him. "I wuv that you have such a big wadder." The lilt of her little voice made him feel bigger. Better. Stronger. "And it weaches almost to the sky. You are so tall!"

He couldn't help but grin back. "Thank you."

The littler girl kept her gaze averted, but she peeked sideways as if to check things out.

Then promptly ducked her head again.

"Thank you for your very kind offer," Devlyn told Biddy. "It will give me a leg up, and that's huge when you're restarting a business."

"My thoughts exactly. You gals have a good day, now." Biddy smiled down at the two little girls. "Soon it will be nice out and we'll put up the swings proper-like."

"They'll love it." Ignoring him, Devlyn smiled at Biddy and steered the girls toward her car.

Halfway there, the older girl turned back, waved and shouted, "Hey, mister, 'member what I said and be so careful, okay?"

"Will do," he called back. "I appreciate the concern, young lady."

She giggled.

His heart didn't usually react to cute kids. He'd have called himself immune, but that all changed two days ago when he caught sight of his very own son.

His heart had gone into meltdown then and seemed to be significantly softer now.

Devlyn got the girls into the car, fastened each one into a car seat, climbed in and drove off without a glance.

He wanted her to see him. Acknowledge him. And when she didn't, he had to face the fact that it mattered to him. A lot. And that put another chink in his armor.

Chapter Five

Rye was helping Biddy.

The kindness of his actions should soften her heart.

It didn't.

If anything, it felt like he was intruding on yet another part of her life, and she didn't need that. Biddy Taylor had been her friend and mentor for years. She'd been a voice of comfort and reason when Devlyn's mother turned a cold shoulder to her while heaping favor on Jed.

She'd made mistakes, yes. Who didn't?

She'd gotten through the last years of her mother's life knowing God had forgiven her and wishing her mother would do the same, but that never happened.

And now Biddy was working with Rye.

Biddy didn't know that Rye was Jed's father. No one knew until she'd poured her heart out to Jess the day before. But it would come out eventually. The town gossips would do their work.

He'd already taken a stance about meeting Jed and he was next door, so it wasn't like she had much choice.

The girls chattered to each other in the back seat. Their lilting voices added sunshine to the spring day. Their great-grandmother had been injured in the fire. Her lungs had been compromised to a point of no return when she'd heroically saved the girls' lives. For now, folks were stepping up, helping care for the little ones so that Hassie and Ed Trembeth didn't lose custody.

Izzie was a talker, and little Beth was just beginning to speak, so big sister did most of the talking and was able to carry on a one-sided conversation. Watching them brought in grocery money, which meant that there would be no grocery money for a while.

She couldn't think about that. Or her empty cupboards. The food pantry had scheduled a drive-through grocery pickup at the elementary school. It was being done during the week, while school was in session.

Would it embarrass Jed to see her car in the line? Would it be visible from his classroom?

She hoped not. He'd worry to think they needed free food. She'd made it through the fire and its aftermath with a mantle of hope for the future, but Jed had awakened crying in the night more than once. Fires were scary, and what child wouldn't be alarmed by what had happened to his home and his town? Adding a lack of food to Jed's worries couldn't happen.

By the time she tucked the girls in for

their naps, two loan applications had come back with refusals.

Jess Bristol called her late that afternoon. "How's it going?"

"Bad to worse, but that simply means it's got to get better, right?"

Sympathy laced Jess's reply. "Oh, Dev, I'm sorry. The loans?"

Jess's fiancé, Shane Stone, had gone over Devlyn's loan applications, making sure her venture sounded strong, but Kendrick Creek had always been a drive-through town. Shane was helping transform it into a more tourist-friendly kind of place, but there was no proof that his efforts would pay off, and banks wanted to make money. Not lose it. "I'm hoping one of the loan companies will see the value in it if we don't get a bank on board. The interest is higher, but your mom's low rent offsets that."

"My mom is this side of a fresh-fried pie," replied Jess. It sounded good to hear her old friend use an expression like that. Jess's two decades in Manhattan had changed the way she talked, so hearing the Southern metaphor made Devlyn smile. "Shane will pick up the kids at five thirty, if that's all right. And you're okay doing a last-minute wedding check with me tonight?"

Shane was watching Jed while Devlyn and Jess put the finishing touches on the plans for Jess and Shane's upcoming wedding. Time was of the essence. Jess wanted her mother there, and Mary Bristol's cancer prognosis was grim, so they'd wasted no time. The April wedding was the following Saturday, and Devlyn was standing up for her childhood friend. "It's all good."

"Perfect. Do you want Shane to drop Jed off back at the cabins? He'll be glad to do it."

"That will save us twenty minutes, so, sure."

Dina Margolies came by for the girls as planned, Shane picked up his kids and

Jed, and when Mary and Jess got home twenty minutes later, Devlyn had Jess's wedding gown hanging from a doorway.

Mary Bristol took one look and teared up.

"Oh, dear." Devlyn grabbed tissues and handed them off. "If this is how you react just seeing the dress, what are you going to do when Jess has it on, Mary?"

Mary laughed, dabbed her eyes and sniffled. "I never thought I'd see this day, and now I am, and it's wonderful. That's all."

"It will be a lovely day." Jess put a pod in the machine and set a cup of coffee to brew. "Anybody else want coffee? Southern sweet tea has not diminished my New York love of coffee."

"Drink quickly or let it cool because we need this fitting done and we don't want coffee stains on this dress."

"On it." Jess left the coffee to cool, slipped into the no-frills gown and stood on a small stool while Devlyn pinned the hem. It didn't take long. Once done, the three women drove to Sevierville to finish off Jess's list for the wedding.

Devlyn got home to the cabins by eight thirty and Shane dropped Jed off a few minutes later. Jed was tired, he'd struggled with geography homework, and he wasn't in a good mood. When he asked for a bedtime snack, she realized they had absolutely nothing in the cabin. She'd meant to stop and grab a few things, but hadn't done it, and all she had were two sticks of gum in her purse.

"We don't have anything?" Jed stared at her, doubtful. "There's always something, Mom. Isn't there?"

There had been, before the fire. Before she'd lost everything. Before her source of income disappeared for months. "I couldn't get to the store today, honey. Sorry."

He looked at her, then the cupboards, and then the empty refrigerator. Her throat convulsed as he swallowed back tears. "I don't think we've ever had nothing before. Have we?"

She put an arm around him. He wasn't starving. Shane had given them a good meal, and the bedtime snack was more habit than necessity, but she hated the lack of options. At this moment, she didn't like the state of her life.

It wouldn't be like this forever.

She knew that. Believed it. But that didn't make it easier on a nine-year-old who was always hungry. "It's different in a house, isn't it? Because you stock up on things in a kitchen. That's a lot harder to do in a small cabin."

His silence magnified her guilt. If only she'd thought to stop for a small block of cheese and some crackers, but she hadn't.

He trudged off to bed like the world was coming to an end.

Just then, Devlyn heard a pizza delivery car pull in next door. Its arrival highlighted the difference in their lifestyles. Rye could order food dropped off on a whim.

She couldn't even afford daily staples.

She pretended not to notice, but when a knock came at her door a minute later, she jumped up and crossed the room, surprised.

The young driver handed her a to-go box. "Here you go, ma'am. Compliments of next door." He gave her a little salute and hurried away.

Jed poked his head out of the small bedroom. Biddy had given them a two-bedroom cabin, but with tourist season coming up, Devlyn couldn't stay here rent-free much longer. Not in good conscience. The Red Cross had helped initially, then Biddy had refused rent once their subsidy expired, but it would be wrong to take advantage of Biddy's generous heart.

Before she could answer, Jed's brows shot up. "That smells so good, doesn't it?"

Her mouth watered at the scent of rich

marinara sauce, but she couldn't accept a gift from Rye. Worse, he knew he shouldn't do this, and—

"Oh, man, Mom, open it, okay?"

The look of excited anticipation on Jed's face forced her decision. She didn't want to be indebted to Rye, but she couldn't ignore her son's hunger. She crossed to the small table and lifted the lid.

Mozzarella sticks with a side of marinara.

He remembered.

Her throat went tight.

Jed's eyes opened wider. "I haven't had these in forever! Do we need plates?"

She shook her head.

"This is the best, Mom! Thank you! Thank you so much!"

He thought she'd done it. He thought she'd ordered unaffordable food to satisfy his hunger, and she could either let him go on thinking that or tell him the truth.

Truth won.

"I didn't get them for us, Jed. The guy next door did."

Jed frowned. "Why would some random person get us food?"

It was the perfect opening, an ideal segue into why Rye would buy him food, but even as she recognized it, the look of pure joy on his boyish face made her stay quiet.

It was bedtime. Explaining Rye to Jed at this time of day would be a fool's choice. He'd never sleep. Neither would she. Opening that Pandora's box of information would have to wait for another day. Fortunately, Jed's preoccupation with the food made him forget the question.

"Aren't you having any?" Jed asked as he lifted a fourth mozzarella stick. "Mom, you have to eat, too."

"I had a big lunch," she assured him. "You eat them."

"You have to have at least one," insisted Jed. He frowned. "You love them,

Mom. You said that at Christmas, re-member?"

She'd always made Christmas Eve a night for foods they didn't normally have, and mozzarella sticks topped the list. The food didn't have to be fancy for a growing boy. It just had to be special, and that made the sacred evening even nicer.

It had stayed that way until the fire hit three days later.

"Okay, I'll have one," she told him, and she lifted the second-to-last cheese stick. She dipped it into the marinara and took a bite.

Delicious.

She wanted to dislike it because it came from Rye.

She couldn't. And she couldn't dis-count the kindness of the gesture. Was her lack of funds that obvious?

Probably.

Most times she didn't care. A lot of folks in Kendrick Creek wore hand-me-downs or shared things from closet to closet. It was no big deal.

But if Rye realized how broke she was? That was a big deal. Would he use that to his advantage to try to get custody of Jed? Would he see her as an easy target for a legal case because she had no money?

But you could have money. You could be comfortable. Seventy-five thousand goes a long way here.

"Isn't this so good, Mom?"

Jed shouldn't have to worry about where his next meal was coming from. He could wear hand-me-downs, but she should be able to buy him his own shoes. His own backpack.

"I'll tell him thank you in the morning, okay?" Jed hopped up, more energized than he'd been ten minutes before. "I'll brush my teeth again, but that's okay because that was the best bedtime snack ever!"

Jed raced her way and hugged her.

"G'night, Mom!" Then he hurried off to bed in a very different frame of mind than he'd had fifteen minutes ago.

The simple kindness had made a stunning difference in the boy's outlook. A kindness from the father he'd never met. Her fault, totally.

She tucked him in, then turned off the lights. From the shadow of her darkened cabin, she peeked out the window.

Rye's lights were still on.

Should she walk next door and thank him?

No.

She'd thank him in the morning. And then she'd set up Biddy's sewing machine, gather supplies and get to work on the pillow design she'd created. Right after she took her place in the food pantry line at Kendrick Creek Elementary.

She swallowed hard.

The thought of Rye's offer hit her square.

Did it matter where the offer came

from? She knew she had to sell her land to finance their new beginning, so did it really matter to whom?

Only if she dug her heels in to get even with a man who never knew he was a father because she never told him. And that put the onus squarely back on her.

Rye wasn't sure what reaction he'd been hoping for when he sent the mozzarella sticks next door last night.

He'd watched his son get dropped off by Shane Stone. Shane had been a year behind him in school and was a convicted felon. That much he remembered. He'd immediately gone to his computer to find out what Shane was doing now and couldn't deny a stab of something that was so like jealousy, he'd be hard-pressed to call it anything else. Was Shane involved with Devlyn?

His internet search showed that Shane was not only respectable now, he ran a construction firm that was a major part of the improvements he was seeing in town. He hadn't realized that Stonefield Construction was Shane's business, and he couldn't deny a glimmer of relief when he saw a brief wedding announcement saying that Shane would be marrying Dr. Jessica Bristol the second Saturday in April.

Next week.

Which meant he wasn't involved romantically with Devlyn.

Don't go there. Trust your instincts, take care of the land. Put personal things on hold.

The mental caution usually helped.

Not this time. Not when the personal thing was a handsome boy with a great smile, a happy personality and his daddy's cowlick. If he remembered anything about being a busy, growing boy, it was the constant hunger, so when the pizza delivery guy showed up with his order, he sent the cheese sticks next door, hoping Jed would like them. Just like his mother had years ago.

Early the next morning, he met Biddy.

Jed was waiting for the bus at the curb. Devlyn came out of her cabin to watch him get on, and when the bus rumbled off a few minutes later, she came their way. He tried not to notice the worn toes on the short boots. Or the frayed seams of the lightweight jacket. Or that Jed's jeans were patched at the knee.

"You need that sewing machine now that you've got a free day." Biddy opened the conversation and jutted her chin toward her place. "The house is open, but it's a hefty machine. An oldie but a goodie, you know?"

"All I need is a straight stitch, a zigzag and a serger."

"And some thread," added Biddy. She smiled. "We'll get you back up and running now that you don't have the girls all the time."

Did Biddy notice Dev's quick look of concern?

Rye did, and it would be silly to have Devlyn carrying the machine from the lower house to the cabin next door. "I'll carry it up for you." He pulled off his work gloves and set them on the ladder. "Do we need the car?"

Biddy swept his sports car a dubious look. "You can barely fit two people and the machine in that sweet ride, son. There's a wheelbarrow in the shed if you need it. Or Devlyn's back seat."

"I can take my car," Devlyn told them. "No worries."

Rye put a hand on her arm. "Let me help. Please?"

She met his gaze now.

So pretty. So strong. A woman of kindness and conviction. And she'd still lied to him.

"All right."

It felt like a victory. As they walked around the graveled drive, the softening spring air surrounded them. When they approached Biddy's door, she drew a breath and turned. "Thank you for the mozzarella sticks."

"Does Jed love them the way you did?"

She nodded but didn't meet his gaze. She reached out and opened Biddy's screen door. "He does. We have them on Christmas Eve every year. It's one of his favorites and that makes a special night even more memorable."

"The little things that make a difference."

She moved into a small side room ahead of him. "That's the kind of thing kids remember."

"Is he a good kid, Dev?" He hated to have to ask this about his own son. They reached for the sewing machine at the same time. His hand landed on hers, and for a few long seconds, the feeling of her hand against his seemed right. So right.

She slipped her hand out from beneath his. "He's wonderful. He's got my dad's love for the outdoors, my needs-to-be-helpful nature and your attention to detail. And the cowlick." She added that with a glance toward his hair. "A winning combination."

"We need to tell him." He couldn't pretend it didn't matter.

It mattered a lot.

But he didn't want to mess up the boy's life any more than he had to. "Does he think I'm dead?"

She shook her head and looked genuinely sad. Then she drew a deep breath. "I told him you left when I was pregnant. I didn't tell him that you didn't know I was pregnant."

He hadn't expected the words to hurt so much. The coil of anger he'd tamped down before rose back up. "So the dad gets to be the bad guy and the mom gets the kid."

She gazed out the window, then lifted her brows. "I should have told him."

"Yeah. And me, Dev."

She didn't accept that. "In retrospect, yes. But when a woman gives her heart and soul to a man, when promises are made only to be thrown away, that has consequences, Rye. I fell in love with you but you left me. As you can see, I've raised a wonderful boy. We're doing just fine."

He must have changed his expression slightly, because she drew back. "Lack of material goods doesn't equate desperation. It equates simplicity. And I'm okay with that."

He wouldn't argue with her. Yes, he'd done her wrong. He'd hurt her and he'd done it to intentionally drive her away because he was scared. Scared that he might end up like his father, dying a terrible, lingering death from early-onset Alzheimer's.

Hey, Einstein? It appears your method worked.

"I grew up without a father. His choice, his fault. But I vowed that if I ever had a

child, that child would know how much
I loved him or her. They'd know that
their dad would be there, all the time.
Jed's never had that chance to know me
or for me to know him, and that's got
to change. Legally and morally," he finished.

"Legally?"

He nodded and lifted the sewing machine while she picked up the thread
board. The thread board was a rain-
bow of spectral colors, well organized.
It showed Biddy's love for her task and
her supplies.

"Do you mean custody?"

He pulled back, surprised. "What kind
of a man do you think I am? Do you think
I'd take a boy away from his mother?"

She flushed, but locked eyes with him.
"I don't blame you for being angry, Rye.
And it's hard to know what choices you'd
make, considering the circumstances."

He nudged the loose screen door open
with his hip and made a mental note to

fix the latch for Biddy in his free time. "I want to know my son. To have a place in his life. To be able to give him something I never had until it was too late to matter. That's not too much to ask, is it?"

Eyes down, she made her way down the stairs. The side railing wobbled when she bumped it.

Another fix went onto his list.

"It's not. But I need to tell him. To find the right time. To—"

"To tell him his mom's been lying to him for almost ten years?"

Her gaze went narrow. Then she raised her chin slightly. "Whereas I'd say I'd been protecting him from the man who tossed his mother aside after finding a girlfriend more to his liking on a business trip. But then, that's my point of view. Clearly skewed." She moved ahead of him and didn't take the driveway up to her cabin. She stalked across the wet grass like a tigress hunting prey, and when they got to her place, she pushed the door open with such force that it bounced back slightly.

A girlfriend?

That was what she'd assumed? That he threw her over for another woman? Well, of course, what did he expect when he'd walked away from her with absolutely no explanation?

"You can set it there." She motioned to the small dining table. She didn't look at him. She crossed the room and set the thread board on the sofa. "Thanks for your help."

No eye contact.

Rigid back.

Squared shoulders.

He set the machine down, crossed the room and went out the door.

She thought you found another woman.

That thought scrambled his brain as he walked back to Biddy.

He'd never thought about what she'd take away from his choice. He'd embraced the role of being a jerk, walking out because he needed to, but he'd never considered that she'd assume there was another woman.

There wasn't.

There was only the image he carried in his head of his dying father, his life swept away by the early-onset Alzheimer's that ran in his family. A disease he'd known nothing about until his aunt called him to his father's deathbed on that fateful Kentucky business trip.

He'd dated, sure. Off and on. But he never allowed anything to get too serious because he could never erase the image of his father in that hospital bed from his mind. Only here it was, a decade later, forty-seven years old and he was fine. Absolutely fine.

He'd dodged a bullet so far. He'd lived his life briskly, building a business and avoiding entanglements.

Until everything had changed three days ago.

Biddy gave him a sharp look as he approached, but she stayed quiet as she held the thin ladder in place while he demolished the two rotting soffits. And when Devlyn left in her car two hours later, he glanced her way.

She didn't return the look.

He needed to make this right somehow, but a ten-year lie was serious business. And he knew that if he hadn't randomly shown up in town, he'd still be in the dark. And that wasn't just unfair. It was unjust.

Chapter Six

The urge to see Jed pulled Rye away from work midday.

He pulled off the road just north of the school, not far from the playground and the small athletic fields. He'd brought a coffee—a big one—and his phone.

He wasn't sure if kids still had recess, but if they did, he wanted to see his boy. His son. And think of all that word meant.

A long line of cars snaked a path in front of the elementary school. Two six-wheeled trucks were parked at the front of the line, and as the cars moved forward, a woman with a clipboard jotted something down, and then the two men would happily load boxes of food into the vehicle.

A food line.

All those people, all those cars, in need of basics like food. The cheerfulness of the three organizers lightened the moment, but he couldn't imagine needing to stand in line for a basic necessity. If the long line below him was an indicator, the fire had taken a huge toll on the small community.

The back doors of the school opened just then. He perched his hip on the front of the car and watched. Kendrick Creek Elementary wasn't large, so when the bigger boys came out, he spotted Jed right away.

The boys and a couple of the girls had brought a soccer ball with them. Almost instantly they set up a game, dodging, sweeping, moving the ball up and down the small field, and his boy ran with the best of them.

Jed was good. Naturally athletic. And laughing, even when he missed a ball and the other team scored on a break-away.

Younger kids had mobbed the playground. A few of the older girls were on the swings and some were just gathered in small groups, talking. But Jed was in the thick of an active game, loving life.

Rye glanced back at the food line and saw Devlyn's car, six cars back. Things were so tight that she was there, in line for food, food for his son.

But then, as the next car pulled forward, she edged out of line, turned the car and headed for the exit. She paused at the end of the line, glanced left, then kept driving.

She didn't get food. She was close. So close. But then she'd turned away.

Shouts of joy from the nearby playground brought clarity.

She didn't want Jed and his friends to see her. She went without food to spare Jed embarrassment.

She'd gone without to spare her boy. Their boy. Rye wasn't about to let Jed or his mother go hungry. The very thought was repugnant to him.

He watched the kids play until a bell called them in. They trooped back in noisily, and he watched as Jed held the door for a group of younger kids.

The act of kindness made him smile.

He didn't get back into his car until Jed was inside. He stopped at the grocery store before going back to the cabin, bought a generous gift card and stuck it in his pocket. Back at the cabin, he put the card in an envelope, addressed it in block letters because Devlyn would recognize his script, then dropped it at a tiny post office box up the road. One way or another he was taking the words *food anxiety* out of Devlyn's dictionary. Forever.

* * *

Devlyn didn't want or need Rye Bauer's help with anything.

The irony of having the thought while she was in a car queue waiting for a food handout wasn't lost on her.

Rye had done well. It was evident in everything he said or did, and when she'd researched him online the day before, it was clear he'd climbed the ladder of success.

Would he fight her for custody? He said he wouldn't, but even shared custody would be a huge change in their lives. And yet Rye deserved time with Jed. Her son deserved it, too, so she'd have to draw a deep breath and be honest. It wasn't about money, although she understood the lack. She'd just rung up a tab for fabric, a bill that wouldn't come due until next month. Hopefully a bill she'd be able to pay.

As long as things progressed, she'd be okay eventually. A small loan and a lot of sweat equity were the current tipping points. The need to get back on solid footing made her vulnerable now.

Rye's offer is some pretty solid footing.

The sensibility of that while waiting for her chance at free food couldn't be denied. If it weren't Rye offering the purchase price, she'd have jumped at it.

But it *was* Rye.

Maybe the food line had made her decision for her. Maybe it was the shame of asking for freebies for the first time in her life. Or having her son come face-to-face with their lack.

Or maybe it was simply recognizing the common sense of the situation. Was she letting pride stand in the way of their future? If so, why?

She didn't go straight back to Biddy's. She drove up the rise to her family homestead.

Bobby Ray and his mighty machines had cleared the debris. Other than the basement hole, the lot stood empty, swept clean. Even the swing was gone.

Her throat thickened a little when she spotted the empty branch. She could have saved the swing. Should have saved it. She'd loved that swing. So did Jed. A simple phone call and Bobby Ray would have put it aside for her, but she'd never made the call.

Disappointment welled within her. The swing, the lack of insurance, the loan rejections spoke to her lack of business sense. A few bad decisions had put everything at risk. Even essentials like food.

Show me the way, God. Show me what to do. Help me—

A series of tiny white flags waved in the wind just then. The waft of air was soft and sweet, but those new flags marking Bauer Farm's roadside frontage danced merrily as if a stiff wind buffeted them.

The land. She had a nest egg in the

land. She knew it was useless to ask for money from the trust, even with the dire circumstances of the fire. The two trustees had made sure that extending her mother's punishment was their agenda and they'd stuck to it rigorously.

But the land was hers. And now—

The time for poor decisions was over. Now it should belong to Rye and his development company.

She drove back to Biddy & Bub Cabins, pulled into her parking space and climbed out of her car. The ladder had been laid down outside cabin four. Biddy was gone and Rye's car was parked at the edge of his small porch. She crossed the gravel, climbed the steps and tapped on the door. When he opened it, she faced him. "I'd like to hear more about your offer. If it still stands."

If he was surprised, he hid it.

He swung the door wider. The scent of soap and aftershave mingled with crisp morning air. It brought back memories from long ago. It might be a different soap, but she recognized the same warm, spiced aftershave and it smelled just as good now. "Come on in."

"A neutral place, please."

He didn't hesitate. He hooked a thumb north. "There's a diner toward Newport."

That wouldn't work. Too many people she knew grabbed lunch there midday. "People from town go there."

"Then let's drive toward Gatlinburg. There are plenty of restaurants and cafés between here and there."

She nodded. "Now?"

He didn't glance around as if she were inconveniencing him. He grabbed a light jacket from the hook inside the door and stepped out. "Perfect. My car or yours?"

He was close.

Too close.

And not just because he smelled so good, but because his quick affirmative reaction to her request made her feel important. She couldn't remember the last time she'd felt important. "Separate cars," she said smoothly. She didn't offer an explanation.

He didn't require one. "Let's go."

He was in his car before she was, but he waited for her to lead the way, and fifteen minutes later, they were parked at a mountain-themed café not far from Dollywood. She climbed out and waited while he parked, then waited again while he walked her way and pretended not to notice how ridiculously handsome and self-confident he was.

When they got to the entrance, he opened the heavy door for her. Something else that hadn't happened for a while.

And when she went to sit down, he held her chair out for her.

He's still nice.

Her heart thought the words. Her brain discounted them promptly.

He tossed you over, Cupcake. Five

minutes of manners doesn't make up for that.

Her brain was correct.

She faced him as a waitress hurried their way to take their order. He pointed to the chalkboard menu above the long, narrow kitchen area flanked by dessert displays. "Steak panini and chicken soup."

Her stomach growled.

He didn't notice. Or had manners enough to pretend he hadn't noticed. More likely.

She'd intended to get a simple coffee, but his order and the food-scented air changed that up quickly. "The soup, please. And coffee."

"Two coffees," said Rye. He lifted a brow in her direction. "You still drink mochas with whipped cream?"

"I don't."

"Then two regular coffees are fine," he told the waitress before he shifted his attention back to her. "No mocha? Ever?"

"I've simplified things." He didn't have to know that she couldn't afford fancy coffee anymore. Easier just to do without.

"Sensible."

"Necessary."

He made a face, sipped water from the glass tumbler the waitress had dropped off and set it down. "I expect you've had to make a lot of necessary decisions, Dev."

There was no reason to belabor it, so she simply faced him quietly.

"I hope that selling the land will give you what you need to be more comfortable."

Her comfort wasn't any of his business. She stayed quiet, trying to make him uneasy. If she succeeded, he didn't show it, and that made her wonder why she was doing it. Was she petty? Or justified?

"We don't have paperwork in front of us, but the terms will be simple. Seventy-five thousand, payable to you, minus any liens on the property and legal expenses."

"There are no liens," said Devlyn.

"Good." He looked happy to hear that.

"And aren't you supposed to pay your own legal expenses?" she asked. She sipped water, too, but not because she was thirsty. She sipped it to give her hands something to do.

"I meant yours," he explained. "You'll want a lawyer to go over the contract and make sure it's clean."

"Do you generally try to mess people up by slipping in things that aren't in their best interests?"

"It's prudent for the seller to be represented," he told her. "I'm representing the best interests of SMD. So the corporate interests are first. But there will be nothing shady in your contract. It will be simple. Cut-and-dried."

Lawyers were expensive. Maybe Shane would examine the paperwork. "I've got a friend who can look at it."

"Shane?"

She frowned.

"I saw him drop Jed off last night."

"Ah."

"And then I did an internet search to find out what my son was doing with an ex-con."

Shane was a great guy, but if the circumstances were reversed, she'd have done the same thing. "With some amazing results, I expect."

"He's done some great things. I didn't realize that the construction firm helping the town was his until I found it on the web."

"Shane is one of the good guys."

The waitress brought their coffees. Devlyn added cream to hers, but didn't reach for the sugar even though she wanted to. Rye had always taken his black, but when he laced it with cream and sugar, she raised a brow in surprise.

"I decided if I was going to live on the stuff, a little cream and sugar would make it more palatable." He sipped the coffee and offered the cup an appreciative look as he set it down. "Good coffee. I can get the paperwork done for you this afternoon. With a check."

"A check?" Devlyn didn't hide the surprise in her voice.

"A down payment," he said smoothly. "So you'll know we're acting in good faith."

"Is that customary?" When he hesitated, she sat back. "I'm not fishing for money, Rye. I need the money. Yes. But I'm not looking for a handout."

"Not a handout," he replied. "It's a payment against the final amount due once the title's been inspected and the deed is ready to be signed over. That might take a couple of weeks, and it's silly to make you wait that long when things are tight right now. Dev." He leaned forward. "The fire messed up a lot of places and a lot of things, but mostly a lot of people. I know it takes time to recover from this kind of thing. Not just the structures, but the people. You need to start working, right?"

That was the plan. "Yes."

"Then accept the check, put it in the bank and kick-start your efforts."

It was a reasonable solution. A simple sale from one person to another. But they weren't just two people. They shared a child. "When you put it that way, it makes sense."

The waitress brought their soup.

She forced herself to savor it, but she knew the truth. Other than last night's mozzarella stick, she hadn't eaten in nearly twenty-four hours. When Rye's panini came, she had to work hard to keep from drooling. Why hadn't she ordered a sandwich, too?

His panini was cut in two.

He put half on the soup plate and handed it over. "Save me from myself, please. I don't have time to run or work out right now, and they didn't offer half portions here."

"I'm fine." She wasn't fine; she wanted to leap across the small table for the plate.

She didn't.

"I know that, but I'd hate for this to go to waste."

She took the sandwich and wasn't sure if it was extra delicious because she was so hungry or the café's food was exceptionally good.

"Can we talk about Jed, Dev?"

The waitress topped off their coffees as he posed the question a few minutes later. Devlyn waited until the waitress cleared their plates before answering. "We need to."

"I want him to know who I am."

She winced inside but kept her face calm. "I will tell him. I'll need to deal with his anger about keeping you out of the picture, and I hate that idea, but it's cause and effect. Understanding that doesn't make the prospect easier."

"I want time with him, Dev."

This time she didn't hide her reaction. "Time?"

"Time for him to get to know me. Do things together. Have him come to Knoxville. Meet my mom."

"Stay with you?" Other than sleepovers with other local kids, Jed had never been away from her. The thought of him spending weekends in Knoxville, without her, was a wake-up call.

He nodded.

He wasn't wrong to ask for this. She knew that, but what would Jed see? A dad with lots of money, cool stuff and a high-profile city life versus a financially strapped mother, hand-me-downs and empty cupboards. What nine-year-old wouldn't choose the easier life? "I have to think about that."

His expression said her answer disappointed him.

Too bad. He'd disappointed her a decade ago and she'd been at the helm ever since. It wasn't a position she'd give up easily now.

She stood. "I've got to get back to the cabin if I'm going to get work done before I get a busload of kids needing help with their homework. Thank you for this." She jutted her chin toward the busy galley kitchen behind the coffee counter. "I appreciate it."

She walked out, needing time to weigh their options. He wanted a chance to do things with Jed. She understood that. But how was she going to broach this with her son? And would he respect her when all was said and done?

Chapter Seven

Rye wanted to trust Devlyn.

He couldn't.

She'd had her reasons to stay quiet about their son, but she'd carried that animosity for ten years. He still wouldn't know about Jed if he weren't back in town because of the land deal, so what did that say about her?

That she's a mother protecting her child and you intentionally hurt her?

His reasoning had seemed altruistic then. He'd glimpsed a future that didn't just worry him. It downright scared him. A dark future that a beautiful young woman like Devlyn shouldn't have to share. Should he explain?

Yes. In retrospect, if he'd done that ten years before, maybe—

He put a hard stop on that thought. He'd had his reasons. He hadn't gotten sick. He'd stayed fine all along, but he hadn't known that would be the case back then. He went with his gut. And maybe his fear. In any case, resigning Devlyn to years of taking care of an invalid hadn't made the short list.

He pulled out his phone once the purchase offer was filled out and texted her. Paperwork ready. Can I come over?

Okay, she texted back.

He picked up the sales contract, crossed to her cabin and knocked on the door.

"Come in."

She said she'd be working. He didn't know what that meant, but when he walked into the cabin, flat folds of material sat atop every horizontal surface, while neatly stacked piles of large fabric squares were bagged and tagged with people's names. He looked around, then crossed the room to look at the pictures she'd taped onto the cupboards. "You make things like this?" He pointed to pictures of displays. Pictures taken on the broad McCabe glassed-in front porch. Pictures that included the kind of things the firm's Knoxville stager used to deck out model homes.

"Me and several others. Anything folks see online or at a shop, we re-create in a handmade version. So yes, quilts." She pointed to one display. "But they're labor-intensive. Your grandmother made quilts for us. She had a great eye for piecing."

He felt bad for not knowing that Grandmaw had left behind a big piece of her life when she'd moved to Knoxville.

"Pillows. Throws. Baby blankets and crib sets. Kitchen things. Things with a Southern farmhouse flair. Mountain decor. We're a team, but I ran the shop out of my parents' house because we had the space and the best location. Lots of folks meander down Kendrick Mills Road when they come north out of Pigeon Forge."

Rye didn't know much about sewing, but he knew the value put on handmade goods was sizable. There was an art tour filled with cottage industries like the one Devlyn had, tucked between Gatlinburg, Pigeon Forge and Kendrick Creek. People flocked to them during the tourist season, which would be in full swing soon. "Did you have an insurance rider to cover at least part of the loss?"

She set down something that looked like a pizza cutter. "The lack of insurance was an error on my part."

He'd thought her circumstances were tough before. They just nose-dived by a substantial degree. Her work gone. House gone. Shop gone. And nothing insured. How was she going to take care of Jed?

"It was a stupid mistake."

Her admission made him swing around. He shook his head. "It was a calculated risk," he corrected her. "I understand. I've gotten where I am by taking risks. All entrepreneurs do that. I'm sorry yours didn't work out, but you saved Jed and yourself. Everything else is replaceable." Replaceable with money, which his land deal would provide. He raised his hand. "Are you ready for the contract? We can do this later if you want."

"No, now is good. I don't have to be at Mary's house for an hour. The kids get dropped off there," she explained. "I'm watching Shane's kids at Mary's because he's been in a cabin up the road and there's not much to do inside the cabins. Outside, yes, now that the weather's improving. But it's an indoor space with limitations."

He couldn't disagree. "They are sparse. Functional, but kind of stark."

She reached for the contract. "I'll see if

Shane can go over this tonight. Is there anything I should be aware of?"

"I didn't sneak visitation rights into the fine print, if that's what you mean."

He regretted the words as soon as they were out of his mouth.

"First thing I was going to check for," she replied smoothly. "I'll check this out later."

That was his cue to leave. "If you have any questions, I'm right next door."

"You sure are." She didn't sound happy about that, but she wasn't combative. Rye counted that as an improvement, but in the end, this wasn't about Devlyn's feelings.

It was about meeting the boy with a quick smile and a knack for soccer. Getting to know him. And loving him. Devlyn would have to deal with that on her own.

He heard her car pull out about an hour later. He'd just wrapped up an online meeting when a deep bark sounded outside his door.

He crossed the room and looked out the window.

A broad-chested German shepherd sat upright on his small porch. The dog's gaze shifted to Rye as soon as he moved the curtain. Then the dog studied him, patiently waiting.

Rye didn't hesitate. He'd loved dogs from the time he was a kid. He opened the door and stepped out.

The dog won Rye's heart when he lifted a paw in greeting.

Rye bent and accepted the gesture. He shook the dog's paw, then set it down. He bent low and gave the dog a good scratch behind the ears. The shepherd's happy expression was enough reward. He'd just straightened when a voice called out from across the yard. "Lou. What are you doing goin' on over there and pesterin' folks? You know Miss Biddy can't have a strange dog prowlin' here and there with renters. Her insurance would go sky-high."

It was the old fellow he'd seen walking the dog in town. A familiar man upon closer inspection. Older now, and not as squarely built. "Deputy Wayne?"

"None other," the old-timer replied. "Who've I got the pleasure of seeing? If you were a troublemaker, I'd recognize you right off, because I saw them kids on a regular basis. The good ones slipped by me sometimes."

"Rye Bauer."

"Up the mill road."

"Yessir." He reached out a hand and the former deputy took it. "Good to see you. You taught some solid lessons back in the day."

"Some listened." The retired lawman smiled. "If you can make a difference to some, that's all the good Lord asks, I reckon. You're back in town, then?"

The dog nudged his way beneath Rye's hand in a silent request. Rye complied and scratched the dog's head. "Doing some real estate."

"The subdivision thing."

"Yes."

"Well, you've got some folks happy, some folks not so happy and some that don't care one way or another," said Wayne. "Miles has been talkin' 'bout it to pretty much anyone who'll listen. To hear him tell it, development is the next big thing, better'n sliced bread. If it's his land you're buyin', it makes sense for him to jump on board, I guess. But if not, he's not an easy fellow to be around. Crosses easy and gets a bee in his bonnet real quick. Come on, Lou." He pretended to scold the dog for breaking through the electronic fence, but there wasn't much weight in the scolding. "It's good to see you again, Rye. Welcome back. And nice to see you giving Biddy a hand. I wasn't bein' nosy, but I saw you helpin', and that makes a difference, don't it?"

"As it should."

Wayne reached out and settled a leash on the dog's collar. "Let's go have a wander around the town, fella, and see how things are progressin'. Then we can settle in for a nap."

Rye was pretty sure the dog wasn't as interested in the nap as the elderly fellow, but the dog nuzzled Wayne's hip, then sat, obedient. "He's too young to have been one of your K9 dogs, isn't he?"

"Way too young, and as smart as he is, he flunked out of candidate school. Has a wandering eye, this one, and likes to think he's boss. I keep tellin' him a stout chain'll keep him in the yard, but I haven't had the heart to do it. Some pups have more wanderlust than others, and Lou's like that. We'll see you around."

"Nice seeing you again, sir."

"Yep. Same."

The old man and the dog brought back memories. Thirty years ago, Deputy Wayne had ruled this town with his own brand of no-nonsense wisdom and order. He always seemed to know who was where and who to keep an eye on. In Kendrick Creek, law enforcement knew everyone. When everyone's your neighbor, not much gets left unsaid.

Rye walked back inside.

The warming weather called to him, but there was work to be done now. Then he wanted to spend the spring getting to know his son. Sooner rather than later.

He didn't realize he'd been unconsciously listening for Devlyn's car until it pulled in. He'd had two video meetings, a conference call and had reviewed two contracts for one of their suburban Knoxville projects, but the sound of her car took precedence.

Two doors slapped shut.

His son was close. So close. Funny how the idea of a child hadn't been remotely on his radar. Now the realization that he had a son changed everything.

He thought twice about each decision he'd made the past few days because there was a boy to consider. What would be in his best interests as a teenager or young adult? What would help ensure his future?

Were they having supper?

Was there even food for supper?

One cupboard door had been slightly ajar, and the emptiness of it seemed wrong, but would it be too intrusive for him to send food over again? Would she suspect his motives?

Probably.

But they'd have food. He texted her. Do you guys like Chinese food?

She answered quickly. Mac and cheese night, but thank you.

It was on the tip of his tongue to say that simple mac and cheese wasn't a meal, but he stopped himself.

He'd have lived on that at Jed's age if his mother let him, and he'd turned out fine. The thought of applying adult standards to kid-friendly life was alien to him, but something he needed to figure out because he had a son now. And it made all the difference.

On the one hand, he was glad that they had food for dinner. On the other, he was a bit disappointed that he couldn't help them.

The realization hit him that he needed to figure out how to become a part of his son's life.

But he hadn't the foggiest idea.

Chapter Eight

Shane pulled up to the cabin shortly after the school bus picked up Jed the next morning. He'd brought two coffees. He handed one to Devlyn. "I needed an extra jump start today."

Shane drank copious amounts of coffee, so Devlyn was pretty sure he got that jump start every day. "Contract looks good." Shane set the envelope on the table. "I'm no lawyer, but it's a simple land deal with all the weight on the buyer because they know exactly what they're getting. Prime land with great frontage for a subdivision. I heard Jimmy Costello say he was selling eight acres of his farm just south of you."

"And the Smiths are involved, too. The bulk of the land is Rye's from his grandparents' farm, so he has a lot riding on this. Maybe too much?" Devlyn wondered aloud as she sipped the coffee.

"Or simply well planned to optimize everything," Shane replied. "You said Rye Bauer is staying next door?"

Unfortunately, yes, but she didn't say that to Shane. Because if it was so unfortunate, why did she find her attention straying that way lately? "Yes."

"I'm going to head over and meet him. Maybe he'd like to see what we've accomplished in town. And what my plans are for the future."

"I expect he would."

"Good." Shane crossed to the door. "See you later."

"Thanks, Shane." She swept the contract a look and raised her cup of coffee. "For both."

He grinned. "My pleasure, ma'am."

She heard his truck pull away a few minutes later. Midmorning, Rye's car hummed its way across the graveled drive. Until that happened, she'd been half waiting to see if he'd stop over.

He didn't.

She set her rotary cutter down and lifted the contract. She'd read it the previous afternoon, and other than a few legal terms, it was written in simple English.

She stared at it. Said one more prayer. Then signed it.

It felt weird. Not wrong, per se, but to have kept Rye's son from him and now do business with him seemed at odds. For just a moment, she wondered how this could have happened. Was the land that important to Rye that he'd strike a deal with the woman who'd hidden his child from him?

It must be.

Last night she'd done the one thing she

hadn't done in ten years. She'd googled him and his company. She found good things. And the only people linked to his internet profile were his mother and his late grandmother.

He'd never married.

Neither had she.

But that was of no consequence now. She stacked the freshly cut pillow squares into the car. Biddy was going to distribute them to several different women. The goal was to fill the pillow display with sixty decorator pillows, a task that would take one person a week to complete. With four women working simultaneously, they'd be stitched and filled in a day. Two women were creating mountain-themed fleece blankets, a popular tourist item and fairly easy to produce. The quilts were too time-consuming to do right now, but they'd have some by summer when she could reclaim things she'd sent to other shops to sell on consignment.

Piece by piece they'd re-create the lost business in the new Main Street–style setting Shane and his crew were creating with his design choices. That was a huge step up from a limited display on her front porch, although the simplicity of her porch lent itself to customer comfort.

Shoppers in the Smokies weren't looking for big retail stores. They wanted charming and homespun, and that was what she'd give them.

She pulled up to the front to drop the pillow squares off with Biddy. Biddy wagged an envelope her way. "Came in the mail just now. For you."

That wasn't unusual. She'd had her mail forwarded to the cabins when she and Jed moved in, but this handwritten envelope was different. She tore open the envelope and sighed softly. "A grocery card."

"Well, now, that's nice. And mighty welcome, I expect," said Biddy.

It was nice, but not welcome, because there was only one person who would have done this. "It's embarrassing."

"I don't know when needing or giving a hand ever became embarrassing," Biddy replied. "You've given help to a good many in town over the years. I don't think it's bad that someone returned the favor."

"You think someone around here did this?" Devlyn asked. The thought that it came from someone else—someone not Rye—seemed better.

"Darlin', I've spent a lot of years on the planet understanding that I don't need to know everything about everything. The good Lord puts folks in our path at various times, and when help comes, sometimes it's just best to humble ourselves enough to accept it and be grateful. It makes folks feel good to know they've helped when needed. I'd leave it at that."

Biddy was right.

Anyone could have sent a card to help

tide them over. It was the generosity of the amount that brought Rye to mind, but it could have been someone else. And in the end, did it matter?

Only to her pride. Certainly not to her hungry child. "You're right, of course."

Biddy snorted. She liked being right. "You heading into town to do those windows?"

She was, and if she didn't hurry, she'd keep Jordan waiting. "Yes. I'll see you later."

"Sounds good."

Biddy waved her off.

Jordan Ash was meeting her to help plan the sales floor layout. Jordan understood retail spacing. She'd run the Friendly Dollar until the fire destroyed the building. She parked and spotted Jordan coming her way. "Perfect timing, as always."

Jordan took a pretend bow. "Your wish is my command. I don't have an estate sale appointment until later this afternoon, so we've got lots of time. Do you have keys to the shop? Let me grab one of those bags." She lifted one of the bags from Devlyn's hand as they came around the front of the store.

"Shane left it open for the painters." As she closed the distance between her and the new building, she paused and swallowed hard. "I'm half thrilled, half scared to death to do this," she confessed.

Ever practical, Jordan shrugged. "We're destined to lose one hundred percent of the races we don't enter," she replied. She reached out a hand and pulled open the heavy door. Shane had picked out an old-fashioned trim for the buildings, just enough to give them the Americana look the town had wanted.

Devlyn walked in.

Rye was there. With Shane. He turned and spotted her and his eyes lit up. She had to pretend her heart didn't stutter-step in response, but it did.

Shane seemed oblivious to the whole exchange.

Jordan noticed instantly. From a vantage point near the front window, out of Rye's line of sight, she silently mouthed "wow" and waved her hands as if to cool her face off, because, yes, Rye was hot—even with an additional ten years on him.

Devlyn ignored her friend's theatrics and set the bag of materials on a step stool.

"Rye wanted to see the town," explained Shane. "I'm giving him a quick tour so he can see how invested we are in bringing Kendrick Creek back to life for tourists. Our hope is for folks to rent a cabin and stay here, then travel to Gatlinburg or Pigeon Forge and take the trolley around to all the attractions. While we're all here," he added, "do you mind if I take Jordan across the street to firm up some details about the store renovation we hope to do for her?" He shifted his attention directly to Devlyn. "I need her input before we start planning specs for her space." Jordan was hoping to turn the old hardware store into a general store. The large building would give her ample room for a wide range of goods.

"If I can find financing," Jordan reminded them. "I'm game, but I'm supposed to be holding up material for Devlyn's curtains," she explained.

"I'll help Dev." Rye took a step forward.

The casual nickname lifted Jordan's brows again. "You don't mind?" she asked politely, but Devlyn knew a prying girlfriend when she saw one. Jordan might still look like the most popular girl in school despite twenty-five years of post-high-school life, but she was an ace at ferreting out information and that wasn't what Devlyn needed right now. On the other hand, Shane had given so much of himself to the town since the fire that she wouldn't thwart him.

"You guys do what you need to do and then Jordie can come back here. Okay?"

"In the meantime, I can hold material up for you," Rye chimed in.

Devlyn was about to object, but Shane clapped Rye on the back. "Good. I'll have her back quickly. Anyone want coffee? Or tea? My beautiful bride has both at the doctor's office next door."

"I never say no to coffee," Rye told him.

Devlyn shook her head. "I'm good for now. But thank you."

Shane and Jordan walked out the door, leaving her and Rye on their own.

Focus on what needs to be done.

She pointed to the step stool. "I need you to drape the material up where the curtain rod will be once it's installed so I can make a decision."

"Just hold it up?"

"Basically."

He lined up the stool alongside the

window seat and climbed to the second step. "Ready."

She handed him a length of plain white cotton.

He held it up. His brow creased, but he stayed quiet.

"You don't like it."

Rye didn't alter his neutral expression. "I'm maintaining radio silence."

She studied the white against the white window trim and reached for the material. "Boring."

His quick smile lent agreement as he handed it back. His hand brushed hers. On purpose?

Probably not. She handed him several other lengths of fabric and none of them were exactly the look she wanted. But when she handed him a bold large-check red gingham, she snapped her fingers. "That's it. Perfect, don't you think?"

"I like it."

"Yeah?" She looked up at him as she reached for the material, but he didn't hand it over right away. Instead he came down those two steps until they stood there, mere inches apart, linked by red gingham.

He held her gaze.

She held his.

And for just a moment, her eyes strayed to his mouth. When his eyes did the exact same thing, she knew she wasn't alone in this trip down memory lane. But the trip came to a real quick stop, because it wasn't about just her and Rye anymore. There was Jed to consider. Jed, whose world was about to be rocked because of her.

She took a step back as Jordan came through the front door. If Jordan noticed their proximity or their expressions, she ignored it. "Did you decide?" she asked as she crossed the broad room.

"The red check."

"Love it!" She grinned and turned to Rye. "Shane said he'll continue the tour across the street."

"That's my cue." Rye handed her the material. He didn't brush her hand with his or lock eyes with her again, and she hated that she wanted him to.

"Thanks for helping." She kept her voice casual.

"Glad to."

Then he crossed to the door, and when it swung shut behind him, Jordan whistled softly. "Okay, you need to dish, because the spark that flashed between the two of you could light up the night sky. How do you know him?"

"He grew up down the road from me until he left for school."

"So he's an old neighbor?" Jordan folded the fabrics and slipped them back into the bags. "And what else? Because there's clearly something you're leaving out."

Leave it to Jordan to know there was more to the story. "We reconnected again later. When I was working for the elections bureau in Knoxville."

Jordan lifted her brows, waiting, and Devlyn couldn't keep her secret any longer. "We fell in love. Or I did, at any rate. And he walked out on me the day I found out I was expecting Jed."

Jordan's mouth dropped open. "He's Jed's father?"

Devlyn nodded, and it felt kind of good to have Jess and Jordan both know the secret she'd kept for ten long years. "Yes."

"Walking out on the mother of your baby? What a louse."

"It was awful, but he didn't know I was pregnant," Devlyn confessed. "I had just found out, he threw me over, and I never contacted him to tell him he had a son."

Jordan's eyes couldn't get wider. "He doesn't know?"

Devlyn winced. "He knows now. He knew it the moment he saw Jed, and he wants to get to know him. Wants to be his dad. And I've clearly bungled everything, because my son is going to hate me for keeping him away from a cool dad for nearly ten years. And I'm not sure how to handle that."

"Oh, Devlyn." Jordan gave her a firm hug, then drew back. "It will work out. He seems nice, but then, nice men don't dump wonderful women, do they?"

Determined to get on with her day, Devlyn pulled out her legal pads and a pair of pencils. "I'll figure this out. We'll figure it out," she amended, stressing the pronoun. "If I think too much about it, I can't focus on the shop. On the bright side, Rye's company is prepared to pay good money for my land."

"That will help with start-up costs," said Jordan as she sketched out a large rectangle on the paper.

"And food," Devlyn admitted. "I was in line for a food pantry handout the other day, but then Jed and his friends came running outside for recess and I ducked out. I didn't want other kids seeing his mom getting free food and pestering him about it."

"I didn't know things were that bad, Dev." Pencil in hand, Jordan reached for her purse. "Let me help. Please."

Devlyn put a hand on Jordan's. "You are helping me by getting this layout done so I know how to plan. You've run a store, so your help here is golden. Rye gave me a deposit on the land he's buying from me, and some nice person sent me a grocery card, so that will tide us over. But thank you, Jordie. Your offer means a lot to me."

The old nickname made Jordan smile. "Well, we've been through fire together, chickie. Literally and figuratively, and we've survived. So, let's get down to business here." She indicated the squarish rectangle she'd drawn. "What're your thoughts?"

Jordan sketched as Devlyn talked. When she was done with the floor plan, it looked ambitious but not crowded. "A cubby wall for yarns takes up almost no usable space and makes it handy for customers. Keep tall displays to the outside walls. That gives your primarily female customer base a good vantage point, because most women are shorter. Catering to the likely shopper makes everything more accessible."

"I love it." Jordan's placement complemented Devlyn's creative ideas. "I'll show it to Shane so they do the finishing touches."

"Good." Jordan grabbed her jacket. "I've got a meeting coming up with a prospective client for an estate sale. I never considered the thought of doing something like this, organizing estates, but it seems I'm good at it. And it gives me a first crack at things I might want to use or sell at the general store."

"You handled your mother's, your aunt's and your uncle Carl's estates for them. You practiced in the trenches."

"Who knew that doing a kindness was really on-the-job training?"

She headed out, Devlyn following her with the bags of fabric samples.

Rye's car, which had been parked across the street, was gone.

She tried not to ponder that electric moment between them in her shop, when proximity and memory melded into one stretched-out moment of temptation, and yet she couldn't think of anything else.

Because she'd almost kissed Rye Bauer.

Chapter Nine

I almost kissed Devlyn.

The thought of almost kissing her only made Rye think more about kissing her, but that wasn't his purpose here. And there was Jed to think about, a boy he'd never had a chance to know because of Devlyn's choices.

You walked away. You deliberately left her. You accomplished your goal. Maybe too well.

Keeping a secret like this had major repercussions for him and Jed. Repercussions that didn't cause mere ripples. They spawned waves.

He finished his tour around town with Shane, called Roseanne back in Knoxville and gave her a double thumbs-up. "This town has pulled out all the stops, Roseanne. Not only is the contractor investing in rebuilding the town, the business owners and landlords are working together to help one another. We're talking a major upgrade."

"That's Smoky Mountain enthusiasm for you," Roseanne replied. "Have you met with that Conrad man yet? Bodie's taken two calls from him. Seems Conrad is anxious to have his parcel considered for development." Bodie was a planning assistant on new projects. The younger man helped clear the path by smoothing out details.

"We spoke briefly. If we decide to do a Phase Two, we could include Conrad's parcel, but that depends on our initial success. The town's resurgence is pointing us in the right direction, but you and

I like to be prudent. That's what's kept us growing so far."

"He won't like that," she replied. "Bodie says the guy is pressing hard. He might be that *special, special* neighbor we run into on almost every job."

The term "special, special neighbor" was their code for the person who would do anything to make sure change didn't happen and delayed projects interminably. "Bodie's reading him well. I'll see if I can be the peacemaker by talking to him about Phase Two. From what I'm seeing here, I don't think we'll have any trouble selling out Phase One in twenty-four months. Low taxes, proximity to the Smokies, the national park, the tourist areas and Dollywood, all with a peaceful view of English Mountain. Total win."

"Your diplomacy's worked wonders before. But it wasn't too hard to walk down memory lane there?"

Roseanne's question startled him until he realized she meant the farm and his grandparents' house. Not Devlyn. No one he worked with now in Knoxville knew about Devlyn. Except his mother. "I got a well-deserved mental smackdown when I realized I should have cleaned out Grandmaw's house before the fire hit. There were some things I'd have liked to have, so that wasn't my brightest move. But Mom's got some stuff, so it wasn't all lost."

"I'm sorry, Rye."

He was, too. He'd delayed because of Devlyn. If he'd come back to Kendrick Creek sooner, he might have discovered his son years earlier. He swallowed regret. "Me, too. Live and learn."

"Keep me updated. We've got three new offers on the Country Cove subdivision here. With the weather easing, folks are making appointments to see the plans and the layout. I think we might sell out by summer."

Country Cove was a hillside suburban Knoxville development. Interest in it was mushrooming. Seven years ago, they'd been a fledgling company, following in the footsteps of the man they'd worked for once he retired. To see their ongoing real estate developments and investments shine was a testimonial to their mentor. And honest dealings.

Rye touted honesty. Espoused it. And yet he'd cast Devlyn out by being totally dishonest. And she'd returned the favor.

He needed to be up-front with her. No matter what else happened, he needed to begin his relationship with his son on truthful footing, and that meant he must explain things to Jed's mother. He owed her that.

He took care of some legal paperwork with the town and drove back toward the cabins, hungry.

Kendrick Creek needed a restaurant. A diner. Something.

And just as he thought that, the scent of wood-smoked barbecue wafted across the road.

His mouth watered.

He did a quick U-turn and headed back. Just beyond the town offices was an empty parking lot in front of a sizable but also empty building. Tucked on the left side of the lot was a big oil drum–style barbecue pit and two smaller pits nearby. An older man was tending the large pit while the smaller pits trailed meat-scented smoke into the air.

Rye pulled in, parked and got out. The sun broke through the clouds just then, and the combination of warm sun and freshly smoked meat made him feel at home. "The smell turned me right around," he told the older fellow.

"Good 'cue'll do that." The man touched the brim of his hat. "Hidey Jones. Nice to see you."

"How soon until it's ready?" asked Rye.

"'Bout an hour. You live far?"

"I'm staying up the road. At Biddy's place."

"She's a great gal, that Biddy. Knows stuff."

Rye smiled because that was high praise coming from a mountain man. "Well, that smell tells me you know stuff, too. How about if I get three dinners to go later on?"

"Come after four, the taters will be set then. Or mac salad. Ginny up the road makes the mac salad and it's solid."

Good slathering sauce and macaroni salad were cornerstones of Southern barbecue. "Corn bread?"

"Yessir. And that cheesy rice folks like so well."

"What do you do if it rains, Mr. Jones?"

"Call me Hidey," the older fellow corrected him. He bent and checked the temperature alongside the smaller smoker, though still generous by normal standards. He jerked his head toward the nondescript building. "Shane Stone's got a plan for doing something here once he's got some other things done. Not fancy, you know. Good 'cue don't hold with fancy, and that's a fact. The fire took just about everything I had for the business, but now I'm goin' again, step by step. I figure we can pitch a tent or two to get by if need be till stuff's fixed." He jutted his chin toward the smaller outdoor oven. "With just a small fire goin', this one works for them side dishes I was talkin' 'bout."

"Is it okay if I come back around five thirty?"

"I'll have 'em ready. But take a chunk of this now." Hidey spread a hunk of some sort of bread with a pat of butter and handed it to Rye. "Nothing like Grandma's good bread to tide ya over."

In the city, he'd have thought it odd to have someone just hand him a thick slice of buttered bread, but it seemed right here. When he bit into the bread, the texture and flavor won him over. "Barley?"

Hidey winked. "I'm not sayin' there is or there ain't because it's not my recipe to share, but it sticks to the ribs, if you know what I mean."

"I do." Grandmaw used that phrase when he was little, and as he drove back to the B&B Cabins, the taste of the bread took him back to a time when he was one of the big boys riding bikes up and down Kendrick Mills Road and Devlyn was a pigtailed kid, watching from the swing.

The swing.

He needed to get it cleaned up. That was a tricky business because the old swing was tucked in Granddad's barn and the fire had ruined the electrical connections.

He'd do it by hand.

He ordered the coarse-grade sandpaper he'd need, some new rope and some water sealant. He might not have much in the way of history to pass on to his son, but that swing linked their families together. That made it doubly important.

He texted Devlyn at a little past four. I ordered three barbecues from someone named Hidey Jones on the other side of town. I was hoping you, me and Jed could eat together.

There was no answer for nearly a quarter hour and he was afraid he'd be eating barbecue for days, but then his phone buzzed a reply. Jed loves barbecue.

Like father, like son, thought Rye. Good, he wrote back. Picking it up around five thirty.

We'll be home by quarter to six.

Perfect timing.

He picked up the barbecue and got back to the cabins just as she and Jed were exiting her car. Jed had a backpack slung over one shoulder, and the tilt of his head, the crooked smile and the blatant cowlick reminded Rye of the mirrors of his youth.

Rye reached for the to-go containers from the passenger seat.

"Do you need help?"

He turned and looked straight into his son's eyes.

His heart skipped a beat. Maybe more than one.

Jed had Devlyn's eyes, an almost sky blue with tiny points of pale light around the pupil. His hair color was Devlyn's, too, but the look on his face took Rye back in time.

"Help would be great."

"Mom! Are we eating in our cabin?"

Devlyn had taken a few bags of things into the cabin. She came out and faced Rye. "I've got material everywhere right now until I sort it out."

"My cabin's virtually empty."

She glanced from him to the boy, then swallowed hard. "Then let's eat there."

He thought it would be awkward, but when they laid out the cardboard containers, Jed's excitement took center stage. "Did you know that Mr. Jones has the best food of anyone up and down the road, even as far away as Newport?"

Rye shook his head. "Is that a random fact or public opinion?"

Jed laughed. "I think it's a fact if everyone agrees, right?"

"Can't argue against the opinion of the masses," remarked Rye.

"Not when they're right," said Devlyn. "This brisket is the best I've ever had."

"Mom makes really good barbecued chicken, like the best ever, and we had an old grill at our house, and she said an old grill was best for slow-cooking chicken because it locks the flavors in, and who wants to mess up a new grill, anyway?"

"Words of wisdom." Rye met Devlyn's eyes across the small table. "Was that the grill your dad had when we were growing up?"

"You grew up here?" Jed's brows shot up.

Rye nodded. "Just down the road from your place. The old farm."

"Me and my friends were always scared of that house because it was empty for so long."

"I should have come back and taken care of it."

"It was my dad's grill," Devlyn cut in. "When the gas parts rusted out, I tossed them away and used charcoal or wood. It served its purpose. There's something about a seasoned grill that brings its own flavor to food."

Making do. Getting by. Scraping out a living while raising a child on her own. Some would find that inspirational.

Not him.

Not when he'd been barely an hour away but kept in the dark. Did the boy resent his absent father? Hate him?

"Mom says you're buying our land to build some houses on it, and that it will be real pretty when you're done." Jed swiped a piece of paper towel across his mouth in a quick gesture, but didn't stop talking as he plowed further into the platter of food. "And I said that's good because Grandma made sure Mom didn't get a single penny from her will, so when the fire burned everything up, we didn't even have stuff to sell, and how can you run a business and not have stuff to sell?"

The kid had no idea that he'd just dropped a bombshell about his grandmother's actions.

The boy's words spiked Rye's protective radar. Dev was Molly McCabe's only child. Who wouldn't name their only child in their will?

"Jed," Devlyn cautioned him firmly. "We don't share private business with others or disrespect your grandmother."

"Well, it's not disrespecting if you're just telling the truth, Mom." He didn't go on, but the nine-year-old clearly had his own opinions. "I don't even know why people leave money to a kid that can't use it and don't leave money to a mom that can use it. It doesn't even make a lick of sense. I heard Biddy say that, but then she said, 'You know your mom,' and I guess you do, right?"

Devlyn eyed the boy. "It's not your place to be eavesdropping on grown-up conversations, and while some actions don't seem to make sense, your grand-mother wanted to ensure your future. I think that was nice of her."

Jed's expression softened. Then he reached out a hand and touched his mother's arm. "I think Grandma loved me a lot. She was just embarrassed that I didn't have a dad, but I told her I don't even need a dad because I have the best mom in the world."

Silence filled the small cabin.

Devlyn studied her plate before she lifted her eyes to Rye. Meeting her gaze, he knew what she was about to do. His throat went tight, because how would Jed handle this news? How would *he* handle it?

Devlyn started to talk when a series of sharp barks sounded outside. Jed jumped up. "That sounds like Lou, doesn't it? Be right back!" He dashed out and let the storm door bang shut in his wake.

"He loves that dog."

The change of subject didn't deter Rye. "You were about to tell him." He stood. So did Devlyn. There was no sense trying to eat when the world was falling apart around him. "We need to, Dev. He needs to know who I am. Who he is."

She moved toward the door. Beyond it, Lou barked and yipped in a merry game of cut-and-chase, while Jed and Biddy tried to collar the black-and-tan dog. Lou had other ideas, and Jed seemed delighted to dodge this way and that with his canine buddy.

Rye followed her out. They'd gotten to the gravel drive just as Biddy efficiently snapped a leash onto the dog's collar. "We've got him," she called up to them. "Jed and I'll walk him back to Wayne's. I've got his extra key if he's gone out."

"Thanks, Biddy."

Rye turned toward Devlyn, unsure what to say, but he was done with silence and secrets. "We need to tell him now. When he comes back. There's no reason for him not to know, Dev." And then he went one step further. "There's never been a reason for either of us to be kept in the dark."

She pivoted like a basketball player on a last-second assist and met his gaze. "You walked out on me, Rye. After promising me the moon and the stars and all the sweet things I longed to hear. When you came back from that buying trip in Kentucky, you didn't just dump me. You made sure that I knew there was absolutely nothing between us and that you'd moved on. So whoever she was or is, good for her, but you have no right to lecture me about my son."

The last two words infuriated him. "*Our* son, Devlyn. He's not just yours."

"I'm the one who's taken care of him for ten years. I gave birth to him, loved

him, cherished him and cared for him.
I wasn't the one who walked away. You
just didn't know you were walking away
from two people, not one, and that's because you tossed me over before I had
a chance to tell you. Why would I want
you in my life after that? Or in his? You
had no respect for me, so how exactly
would that have worked, Rye?"

"You could have called. You could
have texted. You could have sent me an
email if you didn't want to have contact
with me, Devlyn. You did nothing, and
you've managed to hide my son for ten
long years. I wouldn't know about him
now if I hadn't stumbled across you here.
He needs to know I'm his father, and he
needs to know right now."

A strangled sound came from behind
Rye.

Jed had returned, but he hadn't raced
around the driveway, scattering gravel
like he normally did. He'd cut across the
damp grass, soft enough to muffle his

steps, and when Rye turned, he knew his son had heard every word he'd said.

And if the look on Jed's sweet face was any indication, the declaration didn't make him happy, and Rye had no idea how to fix it.

"You're my dad?"

The heartbreak and surprise on Jed's face broke Devlyn's heart. Why had she waited? Why hadn't she been honest from the beginning? Was her ego that bruised by being thrown over?

"Like, my *real* dad?"

Hope speared Jed's voice, but his expression told another story.

"Yes." Rye looked as confused and disoriented as Jed. "Listen, Jed—"

"And you didn't want us?" Jed stared up at him and Rye couldn't lie.

"I didn't know about you."

Jed's face went tighter. Sadder. He faced Devlyn, and the moment of truth she'd never wanted to face was at hand. "You never told my dad about me?"

Her throat closed. There was no way to choke out words. She shook her head.

"You lied to me."

She reached for him, but Jed moved away, out of reach. "You said my dad didn't want us."

She forced a response around the tightness in her throat. "I said he walked away when I was pregnant with you." Devlyn couldn't look at Rye. She kept her eyes on her beloved son and admitted the truth at long last. "But he didn't know I was expecting you."

Jed was an amazing child. He was intuitive and kind, a boy with a big heart. The kind of kid who stood tall for the underdog because he had integrity, but right now this wonderful boy was staring at her as if he didn't know her.

"Jed, I—"

"No, Mom." He blinked twice, fast, a sure sign of tears. Jed rarely cried, and when he did, they were generally tears of anger and frustration. "I don't want to hear any more from you, not ever."

Tears raced down his cheeks, and when he reached up to swipe them away, he smeared dirt across his face. Staring at them both, he turned and raced for the cabin, slamming the door not once, but twice, making his point.

Dear God—

Those words usually began a heartfelt prayer, but there was no prayer attached tonight. Just a gaping hole in her heart because she'd betrayed her beautiful child. She'd done it deliberately, which made her choice just as callous as Rye's, only he'd been honest.

She'd been deceitful.

Her chest ached. Her throat swelled. She walked toward their cabin, unsure what to do, but knowing there would be consequences she'd never considered, and all because she'd hidden the truth.

Shame hit deep.

"Devlyn."

Rye didn't sound angry. He sounded worried, but she wouldn't turn and talk now. She didn't want to see the mix of emotions on his face or think about what this would cost her. Her fault. Not his.

But she couldn't discuss it now.

She climbed the steps and went inside.

Anguished sobs came through the bedroom door. She moved to intervene, then stopped.

He needed time.

So did Rye. He was about to take on a whole new role. She had no idea if he'd be good at it or totally blow it, but he deserved a chance to find out.

What she needed was forgiveness. Jed's. Rye's. God's. And her own, because she felt like the stupidest woman on the planet, with no clue how to make this right. And yet she must because there was a brokenhearted boy whose trust she'd just lost, and somehow, someway, she needed to earn that back again. She didn't know what that would entail.

Soon they could move out of the cabin. The two-bedroom apartment above her store was almost ready for occupancy. That would offer the necessary geographic distance, because having Rye living next door meant she couldn't block him out mentally or physically.

She went to Jed's door.

The sobs had downgraded to muffled groans. She put a hand on the knob and knocked softly. "Jed? Can I come in?"

"No. I don't want to talk to you, to him, maybe ever. I just want to be left all alone."

She hesitated, then stepped back. "Then we can talk tomorrow, honey."

He didn't answer.

She moved to the sofa, sat down and tried to think a prayer. None came. At the root of all this grief and sorrow was the lie she'd casually told to a smaller boy. It had seemed justified then, but she realized that it had been her broken heart talking. Not the woman who'd successfully developed a small business out of her home and organized a cooperative of women to keep it stocked.

That woman kept promises and told the truth.

If only she'd handled her personal life the same way.

Chapter Ten

Rye made the phone call he'd been pondering for the past five days, and when his mother answered, he blurted the truth with no preamble. "You've got a grandson. He's nine years old, almost ten, and he's a real good kid. And I never knew he existed."

"Devlyn."

He wasn't surprised that his mother knew immediately who Jed's mother was. She was the only other person from Kendrick Creek who knew about their former relationship. "Yes."

"Oh, Rye. This has got to be so hard on her."

He bristled instantly. "On her?"

"On all of you," she amended, but he couldn't get past her initial response.

"But you said her first. Does that mean you think it's all right that she never told me? That I never had the choice to be a father to my son?"

She remained quiet, and when she finally did speak, her words jarred him. "Think back to your state of mind then, Rye. After you visited your dad and saw his decline up close. It frightened you."

He recoiled slightly. "The option of ending up like that would frighten anyone, Mom, and it wasn't like I could get a genetic test and find out if it would happen to me. There is no test."

"So you reacted to protect Devlyn from having to care for an invalid."

"It was the right thing to do." The words sounded hollow in retrospect.

"It was a move made out of fear, Rye."

His mother hadn't pulled punches when he was young and she didn't do it now. "Your dad's condition scared you. And I admit, it worried me, too, because you and I had no way of knowing if you'd get it, but you didn't wait. Didn't pray. Didn't examine your options or your conscience. You bulldozed your way out of your relationship with Devlyn and into the life of an entrepreneur. Have you ever tried to figure out why that discontent lingers? That no matter what pinnacle you reach, it's never quite enough?"

"There's nothing wrong with being a goal-setter, Mom." Frustration spurred the hairs to stand up along the nape of his neck. Why was he getting lectured when Devlyn was the one who'd hid the truth from him?

"I agree, but when business goals replace personal ones, including the opportunity to live the life you've been offered, it leaves a hollow spot inside, Rye. An open spot, waiting to be filled."

He hated that she hit that target like a bull's-eye, but right now he was in no mood to examine things this closely. "I'm not discussing this now, mostly because it's not my fault."

"It's not," she replied softly. "Generally, there's plenty of blame to go around in situations like this. Then the question becomes, do you wallow in the blame game? Or pull yourself out of the mire and move forward?"

"Gotta go, Mom. I've got a meeting at nine thirty." He didn't say that the meeting was with a couple of Shane's men, and they were going to pull off Biddy's two bad roofs. The weather was warm and sunny, perfect for demo and construction. Raking rotting roofing tiles wasn't fun, but it was a great way to get rid of some angst.

"I love you, Rye."

He loved her, too, but he didn't feel like saying it, so he hung up and felt like a jerk.

By the time they'd scraped the first half of the cabin roof into the dumpster below, the physical labor had calmed him down. They'd gotten a lot done in a short span of time, so when Biddy brought coffee and fried cakes across the grass, the men took a well-deserved break.

A part of Rye wanted to keep going, but refusing Biddy's act of kindness would be rude. When the other two men scrambled down the ladder, he followed.

His foot never made it to the rung.

The ladder swung slightly left as he gripped it, but when his foot sought the aluminum strip, it wasn't there.

The ladder spun and went down.

One of Shane's men—Mark—raced for it, but he couldn't get there in time. The ladder crashed to the ground.

Rye couldn't keep his footing atop the roof's edge. It wasn't a huge drop. They were single-story cabins, but when he tried to grip the roof's edge to gain control as he fell, a sharp piece of drip edge sliced his finger.

His grip slipped.

He fell. Not hard, but when he landed, his head banged against a tree trunk between the two cabins.

For just a moment, he saw nothing. Then Mark was there, kneeling beside him. Biddy and Chet, the other worker, raced their way. "Hey, man. You okay?"

He swiped a hand to the side of his head where it met the tree. "No blood. I'm fine."

"Rye, are you sure?" Worry deepened the lines on Biddy's face. He waved it off and took a breath.

"I'm breathing. Not bleeding. And feeling kind of stupid. I zigged when I should have zagged." He aimed a smile at her because he didn't want her to worry. "My worst concern was turning an ankle, but I didn't land on my feet, so that's all right. Although sitting might be problematic for a day or two."

"You sure you're okay?" Mark's sober tone indicated the construction guy didn't take falls lightly.

"I am." Rye started to stand.

Mark helped him.

Once on his feet, he rolled his shoulders. It was then that Biddy noticed the blood on his hand. "You're cut."

He shrugged it off. "Caught it on the drip edge."

"Mighty dirty drip edge." Chet frowned as he glanced up at the metal strip running along the soffit's edge, then back to Rye's hand.

Biddy echoed Chet's concern. "Head right into that cabin and wash that out. I'll get a bandage and some antiseptic. Make sure you clean it real well, Rye, all right?"

Normally he'd have thrown a piece of duct tape over the cut and be done with it, but easing her worry was important. "I will." By the time he'd cleaned his hands and the cut, Biddy was back.

"Simple's best," she told him. She applied a dab of the ointment to his cut finger, then snugged the bandage around it. "I'm leaving you a dozen of these bandages and the rest of this tube so you can change it a couple of times a day, okay?"

"Thank you, Biddy." He didn't want her worried. Stuff like this happened, and despite a couple of sore spots, they had work to do. "What I need is a solid cup of joe and one of those cinnamon-sugar fried cakes you brought this way. That'll fix me up."

She got him the coffee and even put the cream and sugar in for him.

The other men exchanged quick looks of amusement. Rye was pretty sure he'd be teased when they got back on the roof, but there were two things he knew.

First, he'd get better-fitting gloves that helped secure his grip, and second, he was going to buy Biddy one of those well-made, self-leveling ladders, because even one story up, an unstable ladder was no one's friend.

By twelve thirty, they'd finished removing the roof on the first cabin.

He saw Devlyn's car pull in while the guys were grabbing sandwiches from a tray Biddy provided.

She saw them, too. A crew of dirty guys, a dumpster and roofing tiles were hard to miss. She ignored them because she was ignoring him.

She parked the car. And when she unloaded several folded boxes—cardboard cartons that looked like moving boxes— instinct pushed him to act fast. He trotted across the gravel and met her at the steps when she came back out. She went to brush by him, but he blocked her path and said five simple words. "Dev. Please. Talk to me."

"I don't know what to say, Rye." She stared at the car and bit her lower lip, not because she was about to cry. She'd always done so when thinking, even when she was a kid. "I can't excuse my actions."

Her candor surprised him, and yet it shouldn't. She'd always been straightforward. Open. Honest. He knew that about her and had loved those qualities.

"I can't speak to your choices, Rye, but mine ended up being petty because my feelings weren't just hurt. They were crushed. It seemed easier to write you out of the picture, because I couldn't imagine dealing with years of your disdain or what effect that would have on a child. But I have to admit that I didn't do it to protect Jed," she said softly. "I did it to protect myself. And now I have to pay the price for that selfishness."

She was heaping too much blame on herself. He needed to put a stop to it. "I didn't walk away from you because of another woman, Dev."

Discomfort thinned her lips. "We don't have to revisit that now."

"There was no other woman," he went

on. "There was an unplanned visit to my dying father in Kentucky."

Her brows drew down tight. "You never visited your father. You didn't even know him."

His father's absence had been common knowledge throughout Rye's life. "He walked away when I was a baby and never bothered with me or Mom, but his sister, my aunt Mae, loved me and stayed in touch. She remembered every birthday, every Christmas and every momentous day in my life, so when she called to say that his dying wish was to see me, I did it for her because she was taking care of him. Mae lived just north of Lexington, so I went to see him while I was at that series of meetings in Kentucky. And then I panicked."

She frowned.

He didn't often talk about this, but the images of the helpless man had been seared into his brain. "He was in a real bad state. His cognizance was pretty much gone. He didn't know anyone. He couldn't take care of himself, and he'd been like this for almost two years while Aunt Mae took care of him. When she heard I was coming to Kentucky, she made the call."

"I'm sorry, Rye. That must have been hard."

He shook his head. "I hated that he walked away and didn't bother with us, but I had a good life. My mom. Granddad and Grandmaw. They were always there for me. I had no complaints, except that I knew if I was ever a dad, I wanted to be a great one."

"And I took that away from you."

He came up that second step and gripped her shoulders lightly. "Dev, when I got home from that trip, I knew I had to end it with you. Not because I didn't love you or care about you, but because I did."

Confusion filled her gaze.

"My dad died from the early kind of

Alzheimer's that hits hard and fast when you're younger. The kind that's genetic. He got it. His father had it. And his brother had it. They all got it by their midforties and suffered through years of debilitating illness where they had to be cared for like babies. I couldn't do it." He released his grip on her shoulders and paced the porch. "I couldn't put you through that, Dev. Ever. You wanted a home and a family. But how could I even contemplate the thought of shackling you to a life with an invalid? It seemed self-ish and wrong. I didn't walk away because I found another woman. I walked away because I was saving you from that fate. Only here I am, forty-seven years old and healthy as can be. I let fear dictate my actions. That cost me, you and Jed. So this isn't all on your shoulders. I'm here to take my share of the blame."

Tears welled in her eyes. Tears for him? Her? Or just the whole awful situation?

He motioned toward the boxes. "What are those for?"

"I'm moving," she told him, and the moment she said the words, he knew he didn't want this to happen. "I'm going to move us into the apartment in town. It's almost ready and it will give us space to get used to this new normal. If I'm going to fix things with Jed and put my new business together, I have to be able to think, Rye. And I can't think properly with you next door, hating me. I need—"

He didn't let her finish. Couldn't let her finish, because the last thing on his mind was hating Devlyn McCabe. He lifted a hand to her cheek, not caring who saw. The workers. Biddy. The old deputy's barking dog that seemed to long for company whenever his owner was away. "Don't go."

"Rye, I—"

He shook his head, held her gaze and kept his hand against the softness of her cheek. "I mean it. I know last night was awful, but stay here until your place is finished. We can work this out together, Dev. With our son. The last thing I want is to push you into making choices you shouldn't have to make. Don't run, Dev. Not from me. Please."

She hesitated. For just a moment, she leaned into his hand. And then she nodded. "I'll stay."

His heartbeat slowed to a more normal pace almost instantly. "Good. Maybe we spend some time with Jed together. There's no shortage of things to do along the parkway." The parkway was the multilane highway linking Sevierville, Pigeon Forge and Gatlinburg. Tourist attractions lined the stretch for miles. "Has he ever gone to Dollywood?"

"Years ago. After my mother passed away, there was no money for a return visit. He'd love a chance to go back."

He didn't want to ask this next question, but he did. "Did she really cut you out of her will?"

"Partially. She left me the house and the bills. The money all went into a trust for Jed." Sadness and regret marked her face.

"Why?" He hadn't known her mother well when he was a boy, but she'd seemed nice enough.

"She couldn't forgive the disgrace I brought on the family by having an out-of-wedlock child. She made things tough the last few years. She grew more judgmental. Maybe because she was sick. When people are in pain, they can act out of character, because she wasn't like this before. She loved me. Then it was like a switch was flipped and she couldn't see past my choices."

She made it sound minimal.

The sorrow in her expression belied that.

"She left me the house, but the assets and money were left to Jed, in trust, with two of her friends as trustees. To access money from the trust, I need to apply to them, and the one time I did, they said no. I think they wanted to make sure I learned my lesson. I never applied again and we got by. Until the fire."

"Dev." He hoped she read the compassion in his gaze. "I'm so sorry. You know what?"

She blinked at his sudden change of tone. "What?"

"Let's start over."

She lifted her brows. "What do you mean?"

"If we're going to live side by side, and share a son, I think we deserve a chance to be friends. Don't you?"

She angled her head slightly, her expression softening. "There's no erasing the past, Rye. It is what it is."

"Well, then, we'd be erasing our son, and that's the last thing I want to do." The scrape of a roofing fork indicated break time was over. "Let's have supper each evening. The three of us. We can practice being normal together."

That concept earned him a slight smile. Small, but a good start, and the moment it happened, he realized he'd like to keep inspiring those smiles just like he'd done ten years before.

"I'm in as long as we agree that normal is relative."

"Agreed." He extended his hand. "Shake on it?"

She put her hand in his and he didn't want to let it go. Her hands might not be as soft as they were when she worked as an office assistant years before, but he'd been brought up to respect the work of human hands. Hers were no exception.

She slipped her hand out of his. "Who's cooking?"

He motioned to the small grills standing outside each cabin. "I'll flip burgers if you make something to go along with them."

"There's the leftover barbecue from last night."

"Let's save that for tomorrow," he suggested. "I'd like to start tonight fresh."

"Then I'll throw something together quick." She took a step back. "You've saved me hours of moving time. Hours I couldn't really afford. Thank you."

He tipped one finger to the brim of the ball cap Biddy had loaned him. "See you at supper."

"All right."

He trotted back across the drive.

Biddy was putting a cover on the cookie container. "I'm leaving this for you guys." She indicated the tin as she thrust a peanut butter sandwich at him. "You didn't get time to eat." She directed her gaze beyond him, toward Devlyn's cabin. "This'll tide you over."

"Thanks." He swallowed the sandwich in a quick series of bites, grabbed a to-go cup of coffee and went straight back up that ladder.

His head still hurt, but not like it had a few hours ago, and the prospect of a fresh start with Devlyn eased the worry he'd been carrying around.

He probably didn't deserve a second chance, but the moment he'd looked into her beautiful blue eyes, he realized that even if he didn't deserve it, he wanted it. When she agreed, it brightened an already pretty afternoon.

"You're having supper together? Every night?" Jordan whistled softly later that afternoon. "That's an interesting twist of events."

Devlyn wasn't about to examine any of this too closely. She checked the time and winced. "I've got to get over to Doc Mary's house. The kids will be getting home and I thought I'd get more done here today." She indicated the sales area with a grimace. "The thought of filling all this space with goods is scary, isn't it? It wouldn't have been so bad before the fire, but—"

"You sure you don't want to fill in with

imported stuff to start off?" said Jordan. "You don't want the displays to look too crowded, but you don't want too much empty space, either."

"I'm considering it," Devlyn confessed as they moved to the door. "It's not something I want to do, but it might be necessary. A broker called from Gatlinburg. He's working with some shops there and he's going to show me what's available to get us through the next few months. It's not my dream, but it might be a crucial initial step." She pulled her hoodie on and brought the hood up over her head once she'd locked the door.

The skies opened up. The morning weather forecast had called for a soaking rain midafternoon and they were right. Jordan's car was parked nearby. Devlyn had tucked hers in the church parking lot around the corner. As she raced to her car, her thoughts went straight to the men on that roof. Would they have the common sense to stop working?

Maybe.

But she knew Rye, and if a job needed to be done at a certain time, it got done. She pulled into the cabin driveway, and there they were, Rye and two of Shane's work crew, scraping the last quarter of the cabin's roof into the second dumpster in the pouring rain.

She started to fall for him all over again at that moment.

He didn't need to do this.

He wasn't a construction laborer. He had money. A great job. And she'd looked up his address online. He lived in one of his own developments, a waterfront complex with all the amenities anyone could ask for, but here he was. On a roof, in the rain, raking mildewed roofing tiles for an old woman he barely knew. Seeing him up there, working so hard, made her heart reopen to possibilities she'd sealed a long time ago. She threw together a quick potato casserole and set it in the fridge. She could stick it in the oven when they got home. She had to hurry back out, but he looked up when she drove past the cabin. He waved.

She waved back.

And then she drove to Doc's to take care of their son and his friends.

Three nights, three suppers, and Jed had barely spoken to either of them.

"How do you make a kid talk?" Rye asked Devlyn once the school bus had picked Jed up. "Shouldn't he open up or something? Talk to us? Lash out irrationally? Something to end the standoff?"

Devlyn had brought her coffee mug out with her. She sipped it and met his gaze over the rim of the mug. She looked real cute doing that. Then she shrugged. "Remind you of anyone?"

He cringed.

"We have to give it time, Rye. He feels betrayed. And probably a little excited to have a dad, so if we keep the conversation open, maybe that's the best thing."

"How do we open it further? Faster?" Waiting had never been his forte, and he wanted Jed to know he wasn't a fly-by-night dad. He was in it for the long haul.

"Dollywood."

The thought of it made him smile. "Will you come along? I know Jess and Shane's wedding is Saturday, but we could go on Sunday."

She started to object, but he reached out and took her hand. Held it. "I'd like you to come, Dev. I know you've got a lot of work right now, but I'd like you there. He doesn't know me yet. Not really. And I don't want him to feel awkward."

She looked tempted but not convinced. "Going places together might confuse things in his head. Kids go from point A to point B real quick."

"Or it could simply show our son that he's the most important thing in the world to both of us."

His argument worked, because she acquiesced with a nod. "I'll come, but I don't do spinning rides. Roller coasters, yes. Nothing that spins me in circles. Got it?"

"Got it. Should we tell him?"

"Tonight. It's a good idea, Rye." She gave him credit easily. "A change of venue is a good trail blazer with kids. And him knowing that his parents aren't enemies is huge."

"I don't see an enemy when I look at you, Dev."

She'd raised the mug almost to her mouth, then paused, looking at him. Watching him. She didn't say a word, simply waited, but he saw a spark of anticipation in her eyes, and that spurred him to go on.

"I see an amazing woman who did what had to be done, despite tough times. Who stood her ground when things got bad, so I don't see an enemy when I look at the mother of my child."

Her hand shook slightly. Just enough to

let him know his words mattered. That maybe *he* mattered.

"I see a woman who's grown more beautiful with time. And if you don't mind, Dev, I'd like to get to know you all over again."

She swallowed. "Rye—"

He reached out and lightly touched the back of her head. "Just wanted you to know." He tapped his watch. "Gotta go."

He crossed to his car and realized how out of place it looked sitting there. Like he was showing off what he had, which had been the point when he bought it, but it wasn't the point now.

Jed was the focus.

And if he was honest with himself, Dev was, too, and that wasn't what he'd expected when he took the turn toward Kendrick Creek over a week before.

Chapter Eleven

Rye walked into the town offices ten minutes later. The clerk waved him on to the supervisor's office. The planning board meeting was scheduled for the last Thursday of the month and Rye was here to hand over copies of the Plan A proposal he and Roseanne had drawn up.

He came to a stop inside the door.

Miles Conrad was sitting in the office. He'd turned his chair to face the door so that Rye would see him right off. He saw him, all right. And the look on Conrad's face wasn't pretty.

"Mr. Conrad, good morning. This is an unexpected pleasure."

"Shouldn't be all that unexpected when a man's approached about his land options, then hung out to dry because there's a pretty woman involved. That's not how things get done in Kendrick Creek, young man."

The condescending tone was meant to put Rye in his place, but Rye had worked with planning and zoning boards for nearly two decades. Not much surprised him or threw him off his game. "You're on the planning board?"

"Interim chairman while Mick Hearst is recovering from surgery. That makes me the deciding vote."

That was why Conrad's name hadn't turned up as they'd done research on the town's movers and shakers.

It wasn't the words as much as the tone that tipped Rye off that a tiebreak situation could happen. And if Miles Conrad had undue influence on any other board members, he could swing the vote negatively with relative ease. "Then I'm glad you're here." Rye handed him a copy of the plan, then handed the other copies to the town supervisor. "There are enough copies so that the entire town council will have their own to examine."

The supervisor looked torn, but Rye wasn't sure if it was because of Conrad's animosity or the proposed subdivision. He accepted the folder and motioned Rye to sit. He reached out and shook Rye's hand with a solid grip. "It's nice to meet you in person, Rye."

"Likewise."

The supervisor took his seat while Rye did the same. He opened the folder as he addressed Rye. "I knew your grandmother well. My wife bought two of her quilts for our daughters a few years back. Beautiful workmanship."

Rye smiled. "I appreciate that, sir. Grandmaw was a corker. She did her best at anything she put her hand to and helped raise me the same way. When my partner and I look at areas for subdivision or renovation, we look down the long road. We're not a short-term company. We're in for the long haul or we're not in at all. And the list you have there, of references and projects we've overseen, examples our philosophy."

"I saw that in the preliminary proposal," noted the supervisor. "I appreciate that you're going over things with us ahead of time. It saves time at the meeting."

"Glad to do it," Rye replied. "Answering questions up front is always a good first step. Better that we all go into the meeting with the best understanding of the proposal."

"Which is why I'm here." Miles pretended to study the proposal before him. "What I'm wondering is why we're looking at this upper ridge proposal that robs the town of valuable agricultural acreage when my partially cleared forest land below is clearly the better choice for all concerned."

Rye was glad that Roseanne and Deputy Wayne had both alerted him to red flags around Miles Conrad. The man's animosity didn't blindside him. "Timing and English Mountain," he answered swiftly. "We've all lived here a long while," he continued. "The view from both sides of Kendrick Mills Road is stunning. It's a crowd-pleaser. An elevated view of the Blue Ridge is a huge sales point for a lot of folks and the fire changed availability. It opened up the sale of three parcels. We've obtained all three now, which puts Phase One in the driver's seat, although..." He turned toward Miles. "Your land would abut mine for Phase Two if initial sales are as good as I expect them to be."

The supervisor arched his brows. "But there's no guarantee that Phase Two will happen, is there?"

"Phase Two hinges on sales of Phase

One properties," answered Rye. "Which is why we've started with the ridge land. When I swing, I swing for the fences. Garnering those pieces of land is a home run in my book."

"And a strikeout in mine," Conrad retorted.

Rye disagreed. "I'd say it allows us another at bat in a year or two. We develop, sell, make sure folks are happy, then expand. It's a formula that's worked well for Smoky Mountain Development so far. Happy people are our best advertisement."

"Except I'm not happy, Mr. Bauer." Miles stood and slapped his copy onto the supervisor's desk. "Not one bit. I was led to believe that my land was in the running."

"Which it was. As I said, the fire changed things for a lot of people."

"So you're willing to access nearly eighty acres of farmland to build homes that may or may not sell instead of using wooded land that isn't agriculturally friendly? Our state is losing sixty thousand acres of farmland a year, Bauer. Deals like yours are changing the face of Tennessee and I don't like it. I don't like it at all."

Rye stayed seated purposely. He'd heard the stats before, and while they were accurate, he knew both sides of the pressing equation. "We have people moving here. They need a place to live. So they either look on the west side of the national park, into Tennessee, or they look east into North Carolina. I'd prefer to have all that increased tax base on this side of the state divide. The numbers quoted in the proposal bear me out. North Carolina and Tennessee are running neck and neck. With Kendrick Creek's proximity to the national park and the foothills parkway, I want people to pick the Volunteer State as their new home address. And I'm hoping the people of Kendrick Creek agree."

"You've talked about development for a long time, Miles." The supervisor didn't stand, either. "Would you really get in the way of this project because your land is put on hold? Board members are supposed to be impartial."

"Impartial, yes. Stupid, no. I'll see you both at the meeting."

He picked up the folder and strode out.

The supervisor sighed. "Our timing isn't great," he told Rye. "With Mick out sick and Miles assigned his seat, it might be tough to get this through. Doc Mary was on the board, but she stepped down because of her illness. Hidey Jones took her place, and he's fair-minded, but Yancey Clark sells to the Feed & Seed and buys from them, too. It's going to be hard for him to vote against Miles. Small-town living," he noted ruefully. "We're pretty interconnected here. Still, the planning board is only one step, and I expect the town board will vote in your favor when it comes to us. But it has to get through them first and Miles is going to be a stumbling block."

"He's going to try." Rye stood and extended his hand. "I think the more people we get to that meeting, the better chance we have of getting the approval we need. Miles is running the biggest retail shop in the area. Happy customers are more likely to spend money. And any good retail guy knows that numbers count."

"Except it's the only place to get farm supplies or even backyard supplies between Newport and Gatlinburg, which has kept him in the driver's seat for a long time."

A cornered market of necessary goods. That put Miles in a position of power.

Rye shook the supervisor's hand before he left.

He'd been in this spot before. He'd purchased land in and outside of Knoxville and had eventually used some of those parcels in development. He'd done well with it.

But Devlyn and her neighbors were counting on this deal now. Their properties had been destroyed.

Conrad's business had suffered no damage. No loss. He'd actually gained sales as people needed to replace destroyed equipment and supplies.

Waiting for Phase Two wouldn't hurt anything but Conrad's pride.

For the Costellos, Smiths and Devlyn, the land deal could mean survival. He needed to make it happen.

The question was, how?

The tempting smell of smoked pork chops wafted between the side-by-side cabins that evening.

Bird chatter had intensified as songbirds nested. The greening trees, the lively tulips, the grill scent filling the air at Biddy's and the smell of Hidey's barbecue in town indicated welcome change.

True spring had arrived in Kendrick

Creek. Jed had gone up the back hill to gather ground clutter for a science project. He came back with a pail of bug-infested organic matter. "Mrs. Simms is going to love this so much because she said that some of the best bugs are the ones that eat the most disgusting stuff. They turn it right back into soil and then it feeds the trees all over again. How cool is that?"

Rye was bringing the pork chops over to the table. "The coolest. Except for maybe... Dollywood? This Sunday? You. Me. Your mom?"

Jed's mouth dropped open, but he kept his grip on the bucket. "Dollywood? For real?"

"For real."

Excitement claimed his features, but then he turned to Devlyn. His next words showcased his thoughtful nature. "But you're in the wedding on Saturday and you have stuff to do for the store. You said so."

She reached out and hugged his shoulders. "Have I told you lately how much I love you, kid? You're one hundred percent correct, but Jordan's going to help out with a couple of the ladies so I can be with you guys on Sunday."

"So we can go?" Hope and joy didn't just brighten Jed's face—they owned it. "All of us?"

"Yes."

"I can't believe it!" He fist-pumped the air, then grabbed Rye around the middle in a ginormous hug. It was Rye's first hug from his son, and when Devlyn lifted her gaze, emotion swept her.

His eyes had filled.

He didn't cry, but the tears in Rye's eyes were real. And his expression, like someone had just given him the best gift ever, did a dance on her heart. She was thrilled to see his reaction, but felt guilty because she'd kept Jed from him for so long.

Rye didn't let the situation get crazy

emotional, though. He hugged Jed back, then picked him up, threw him over his shoulder and ran around with him. "We are going to have a ball," he yelled.

"Yeah!" Jed hollered back as loud as he could.

"Roller coasters!"

"Double yeah!"

"Crazy rides!"

"Even better!"

"Junk food!"

"Best day ever," laughed Jed as Rye lowered him from his shoulder. And he didn't do it nice and easy, the way a mother would. He kind of let Jed free-fall, then caught him. It was a trick with a toddler. It was a much bigger trick with a healthy nine-year-old, but Jed kept laughing, even when he almost hit the ground, because somehow he knew that his father wouldn't let that happen.

It wasn't a quiet supper that night. It was positively noisy. Jed asked a million questions about the amusement park. About the day.

They answered them the best they could. He faced Devlyn as they finished. "Mom?"

"Yes?"

"Do I have to go to Jess and Shane's wedding on Saturday?" he asked. He followed it up with nine-year-old reasoning. "Can I maybe not go and stay with Rye for the day? If that's okay with you?" He darted a quick look at his father. He wasn't calling Rye "Dad" yet. Which made perfect sense.

Devlyn looked at Rye. "Are you free on Saturday?"

"I can be." He shifted his gaze to Jed. "My mom wants to meet you. How about we take her to lunch and go do something with her while she's here? She lives near Knoxville and she was pretty stoked to hear she has a grandson."

"I have a grandma again?" Joy and wonder filled Jed's eyes. "I didn't even think of that, that I would have a grandma. And a grandpa?"

"Unfortunately, my father died nearly ten years ago. But my mom is very excited to meet you."

"I'm excited to meet her, too. I would like that a lot. Is it okay, Mom?" He turned back toward Devlyn. "Can I stay here and meet my grandma? And stay with Rye?"

No way could she refuse. "It's fine with me. Although I'll miss our dance at the reception," she teased him, laughing out loud when he groaned. "Stay with your dad, meet your grandma, and I'll be maid of honor at the wedding. It's all good."

"Can I tell Biddy? And Wayne? About having a dad? And a grandma again?"

"Sure can."

He raced off.

She watched him go, then sighed. "This is much better, isn't it?"

"Than sullen silence?" Rye made a face. "I'd say so. Who'd have thought a bunch of cool roller coasters and attractions would have such an effect on him?"

"I think he's as excited about your mom as he is about Dollywood." Devlyn stood and began clearing the picnic table, but broached the topic now that Jed was out of earshot. "Does she hate me? Your mom, I mean."

"Not in the least." His quick reply reassured her. "She reminded me that I acted like a jerk and that women have a sworn duty to protect themselves and their children."

His reply came as a complete surprise. "She didn't say that."

"Pretty much did. It made her point. You're not the enemy, Dev. To her. Or to me. Thanks for letting us do this. I can't remember ever looking forward to a weekend like I am right now. You've made a difference. *He's* made a difference." He motioned toward Jed as he dashed across the connected yards to share his news with Deputy Wayne. "It means a lot."

She saw that in him, but even more in her son. And it felt good. She headed toward the cabin with the dishes. "You're welcome, Rye. I hope you all have fun."

He followed. He helped clear things every evening, as if sharing the kitchen tasks was expected, and that was something else she appreciated. She didn't mind cooking, but a hand with cleanup sure was nice. But in the end, it was one more thing she didn't dare let herself get used to.

Chapter Twelve

❧

"I haven't been to a monster truck show in thirty-five years," Carol Bauer confessed as they watched Jed wait in line for his cotton candy. "And a part of me can't believe why I'm doing it now. He's beautiful, Rye. Absolutely marvelous."

She clutched Rye's arm and he drew back in mock horror when emotion gripped her voice. "Please tell me you brought tissues. Let's not scare him, okay?" He made a funny face at his mother and was relieved when she pulled out a clutch of tissues with one hand and swatted his shoulder with the other.

"I just can't get over it," she whispered, but she swiped her eyes and flashed him an only slightly watery smile. "He reminds me so much of you. Devlyn, too, he's got the look of her, but his actions, his voice, that funny way he pulls his brow down when he's letting you know he absolutely, positively doesn't believe you—it's all you."

"He's a funny kid. And he's smart. I got to see his school records and he's on top of his game. Although he doesn't like geography."

She laughed and hugged Rye's arm. "Most fourth graders aren't in love with geography, but of course he's smart. Look at his parents."

"Can I get a slushy, too?" Jed called over to them. Rye had realized quickly that a nine-year-old didn't necessarily want a parent hanging over their shoulder all the time, paying for things.

"Let's save the slushy for later," Rye called back.

"Okay." He took his cotton candy from the gal behind the counter and held the paper cone high. "I think this is the biggest one I've ever seen. Like for real."

"It's amazing." Carol Bauer smiled down at him.

"Grandma, you want a pinch? I'll share."

His mother acted like it was the best offer she'd ever received. "I'd love it, Jed. And thank you, grandson."

Jed's grin split his face. He hadn't called Rye "Dad" yet, but he seemed fine with a brand-new grandma.

The day went by fast. Dust. Dirt. The sound of revved engines and spinning tires, and the rumble of truck versus truck.

"Kid, this was a great idea," Rye told him later. "I'd have never thought of a monster truck show. Your grandma and I are having a great time. Although we're pretty grimy."

The warm conditions and growing humidity made the dust cling to their skin, but that didn't matter. They were having fun. They would just need a good cleanup before church in the morning. "Where shall we go for supper?" asked Carol. "My treat."

"Mom, you don't have to do that."

"But I *am* really hungry," Jed mentioned, just in case his new grandmother took Rye's admonition seriously. He needn't have worried, and after a Tex-Mex supper at a Newport restaurant, Jed said goodbye to Rye's mother in the parking lot. "I'm glad you came with us," he told her. "I know it was really dusty. And loud. And you didn't even complain one bit."

"I'm quite washable," she assured him.

He laughed and gave her a spontaneous hug. "Me, too!" He dashed to Rye's car, ready to peruse the stack of truck magazines they'd gotten at the show.

"Pretty neat, huh?" Rye bumped shoulders with his mother.

She leaned her cheek against his shoulder and sighed. "What a blessing he is, Rye. And Devlyn's doing okay?"

"She is."

"Is there someone significant in her life? A boyfriend?"

"Not according to her."

"Ah."

"No 'ah,' Mom."

She shrugged. "This gives you both time to adjust to the situation. Jed, too. He's a marvelous boy, Rye."

"Yeah, he is." He gave her a hug. "Talk to you soon. Thanks for driving over."

"My absolute pleasure." She smiled as she went to her car and he waved her off. When he climbed into the driver's seat of the sports car, he noogied Jed's head lightly. "Good day?"

"Best day ever."

Rye's chest swelled. It wasn't a contest. He knew that. But he appreciated Jed's overwhelming approval.

Jed was yawning when they got back to the cabins. The wedding was a daytime affair because the happy couple didn't want to overtax Jess Bristol's mother, so he half expected Devlyn to be home.

She wasn't and he felt a little weird, wondering what to do now. Keep Jed with him? Take him into Devlyn's cabin? After a great day, he had no idea what to do with a kid at bedtime and he didn't want his ineptitude showing. He hesitated just long enough for Jed to take the lead. "Biddy's got an extra key for our cabin. I'll get it."

"I'll come along." He and Jed crossed the grass. The dew hadn't settled yet. The grass held the daytime warmth, another nod toward the warming trend. It felt good to cross the informal lawn with his boy. To hear him laugh. To talk with him. Lou barked a welcome from across his yard, a gentle series of woofs.

When they approached Biddy's door, she opened it from the inside. "Hello, fellas. What can I do for you?"

"Hi, Miss Biddy!" Jed scrambled up

the steps as if suddenly reenergized. "We had the best day! We went to a monster truck show and my new grandma came with us and it was so much fun. I got to see so many monster trucks and the Exterminator and Terminator monster truck war was the best! They even had little trucks come out and try and help the big trucks win. It was so cool! And we're going to Dollywood tomorrow, just me and my mom and Rye, and I can't even believe this! Can you?"

She patted him on the head. "It's wonderful, Jed. Absolutely wonderful. And you're a mess."

He tipped his face up to her and laughed, showing off the gap from a missing tooth on the left side. "I know. I need a shower. Can I have the extra key, please?"

"You sure can." She moved to the pegboard behind the desk and removed a key. "Here you go. I won't pretend it's not a pleasure to see a boy and his dad having an adventure or two. Does my heart good."

"It did my everything good!" exclaimed Jed, laughing. He darted off across the grass.

Biddy wiggled her tightened door latch. "Thanks for fixing this. I tried every which way to get it to meet up proper and nothing worked."

"I shimmed it," he told her. "I painted the shim white so it blends in. We might have the opposite problem when the heat sets in. But if the door swells and latches too tight in the humidity, I'll remove the spacer. It will be simple enough to reapply it next fall."

"Your daddy liked building things, you know."

Rye frowned. "You knew my father?"

Biddy shook her head and stepped outside. She took in a breath of the clean, fresh air and sighed. "No, but your grandmother shared this and that. We gals kept our hands busy, but we weren't afraid to let our tongues wag a bit, if you know what I mean."

He nodded. He knew Grandmaw.

"She said your daddy had a builder's hand and a love for creating, but there wasn't any stick-to-itiveness in him. He would start a job but couldn't seem to see it through. She said that included being a husband and a father."

"I didn't really know him. He left when I was little. My mom wasn't one to talk badly about others. She took the reins and moved forward. But Granddad didn't shrug it off quite so easily, so I heard my share."

"You get your work ethic from your mom's side. And it seems you got the eye for building and development from him, and it's nice how the good things all came together in you. I know he died a sad death."

So Grandmaw had mentioned that. Rye dipped his chin. "Horrible."

"Right about the time Jed was born."

She leveled a steady look at him. "There's turns in life that can set us up or take us down, and the ones that take us down are generally rooted in fear."

His mother had hinted at the same thing and he'd gotten upset. Because the truth hurt?

Maybe.

But also because the truth made him take a hard look at himself and his choices. "Wise words, Biddy."

She didn't smile. She took a deep breath. "Well, you don't get to see the south side of seventy without gaining a few smarts along the way. It's putting them to use that makes the difference, I guess."

Devlyn's car turned into the drive at that moment. She saw them and waved, then continued around the semicircle to her cabin.

"See you tomorrow, Biddy."

"Good Lord willin', I'll be here."

Satisfaction buoyed him as he crossed

the grass to tell Devlyn about their day. But when she stepped out of the car in a slim-fitting full-length black dress, he was stopped in his tracks.

He stared and maybe gulped. He wasn't sure, because the only thing he could think of was how absolutely beautiful she was.

Devlyn stepped out of the car with care. She didn't want anything to snag this pretty dress. "I hope I didn't keep you guys waiting," she called across the grass.

Rye was heading her way.

He paused. And then he whistled softly.

Heat rushed to her cheeks. His look of appreciation only deepened the flush. "Wow."

"Stop it."

"Impossible." He reached a hand to hers and gave her a little spin. "Yup. Wow."

She pulled her hand loose. "Well, it was

a wedding, and the maid of honor is supposed to look nice. But not nicer than the bride. I'm happy to say Jess looked gorgeous." She smiled, remembering. "Did you guys have fun? And did you get the backup key from Biddy? I thought I'd beat you here, but I didn't."

"All good. Jed's inside, either raiding the refrigerator, washing off a generous amount of Tennessee dust or sound asleep. He was exhausted right up until he gave Biddy the lowdown on his day. The retelling gave him a jump start. And my mother has fallen in love with him. She cried."

"Oh, Rye." She'd started for the steps to check on Jed, but Rye's words turned her around. "Is she all right?"

"Happy tears," he told her. "A grandchild she'd never expected. It's all good."

She walked up the steps and through the door, then tiptoed back out. "Sound asleep on the couch. Didn't even make it to the bedroom. Or the shower. He must have had a good day."

"We all did. It was beyond my expectations. Who knew hanging out with a kid could be so much fun?" He motioned to the twin rockers on the small front porch. "Can we sit? Talk for a minute?"

"Let me get changed. Or at least get a sweater."

"Here." He slipped his jacket off and draped it around her shoulders. Then he stood there. Right there. Looking down at her. Locking his eyes with hers.

"I can grab something inside, Rye."

"This is better." He left his hands on her shoulders, his grip strong and true. He smiled at her and then his gaze dropped to her mouth. "Much better."

Electricity thrummed, and it had nothing to do with the dusk-to-dawn lights surrounding the cabin yard and everything to do with the expression on Rye's face.

It didn't matter who kissed whom. The

moment his mouth touched hers, nothing else mattered.

And it was every bit as perfect and wonderful as she'd remembered. Her mind scolded as her heart melted. She went with her heart, because being in Rye's arms, snug in his embrace, felt right, and that was enough for the moment.

Eventually he dropped his forehead to hers. And sighed.

And then he kissed her again.

"This isn't talking," she whispered when he finally pulled her into a warm embrace. "You did mention talking, I believe."

"Kissing got in the way." He pulled back and smiled, then took her hand and led the way to the rocking chairs. "But talking's important. Just not as perfect."

Mental warnings shot up. She'd heard those words before. Were they sincere now? She wanted them to be, but experience said she should be cautious.

He pulled the rockers close together. He sat in one. She settled into the other. "You used to talk about this scenario," he reminded her. "The cozy house, a porch with rocking chairs…"

"And a yard full of kids' toys." She shrugged lightly. "Until now, I've been blessed to have a solid home, a healthy son and enough money to get by. That's pretty good, Rye."

"It is." His expression grew serious. "You've done well, Dev. With Jed. With your life. You've taken care of the most important things. And I'm sorry I wasn't around to help you during the rough spot, after the fire."

His apology made her squirm. "It's hard to be around if you don't know. I should have told you earlier. I'm sorry I didn't."

"If I hadn't run scared back then, things could have been different. For you, for me." He indicated the cabin door and the sleeping child inside. "For him. I told myself I was protecting you, that a real man wouldn't saddle someone with what could be a horrible illness. I knew what you'd say." He exchanged a look with her. "You'd have said it was in God's hands and I'd have caved. But I would have hated myself for putting you at risk like that. It wasn't a life I would have chosen for me, and it sure wasn't something I wanted for you. And in my head, kids were out of the question because why would I want to pass on my flawed DNA? It seemed easier to make you hate me than love me through all that."

"I deserved a chance to make the decision on my own," she told him. "And in case you haven't noticed, you're not sick."

"Very true. I am ridiculously healthy." He didn't hide his relief. "I thank God for that. I'm forty-seven. My father began showing symptoms by forty-five, so maybe I don't have the disease. But after seeing my father struggle with his illness, it seemed easier to be on my own. Simpler because no one was counting on me. But that meant I gave up the best thing that ever happened to me, Dev. You. And I want you to forgive me."

It should crush her that her beautiful son might be carrying the genes for an incurable disease.

It didn't.

She faced Rye. "You said I've done well, and I have, but it's not because of me. Not me alone. And not my faith alone, although that's been a huge comfort. It's grabbing hold of the Serenity Prayer each day. Knowing I can change some things even when I can't change others. And having the wisdom to discern between the two. I can't change your genetics. Or Jed's. But who knows? Science could end up curing Alzheimer's in the next thirty-five years, so why spend my whole life worrying about what I can't change?"

"You're more accepting."

"Now, yes," she acknowledged. "I'm older. I've had a lot of life to deal with the past ten years." She pressed his hand gently. "I'm sorry for how everything went down. And sorry for the time you lost with Jed. But we're here now. And we can be good parents to this wonderful kid. I suggest we leave the past where it belongs and move on. Take the future a day at a time. The way it should be."

He stood and reached for her.

She rose and slipped into his arms. He held her in a solid embrace, then leaned back. "Are we eligible for a do-over?"

"A start-over," she corrected him. "Neither one of us knows where this can or should go. So let's pick up here, okay? And move forward."

"Running?" Hopeful expectation and a splash of humor lightened his voice.

"Strolling," she ordered softly. "No sudden moves. Jed's got enough on his plate right now. We take it slow. Not just for him." She pulled back. "For us. We're not the same people we were in Knoxville. We're older, wiser. And having been a single mom for ten years, I don't risk things when it comes to Jed. Slow and steady is my current pace. And I'm okay with that."

"Slow and steady it is. Except for—" His smile deepened.

"*Especially* for that," she scolded, but hugged him. And then she whispered words for his ears only. "I've missed you, Rye. So much. I've never stopped missing you."

He held her close and said the words she'd been longing to hear for way too long. "I know. Me, too. It's good to be here, Dev. It's good to be home."

Chapter Thirteen

"Guys, this is so amazing!" Jed raced Devlyn's way after a particularly crazy ride at the amusement park the next day. She'd deliberately avoided the spinning ones. Instead she snapped fun pics with her phone. Pics of Rye and his son, bonding. "I can't believe how many rides there are," Jed exclaimed. "I don't remember it being like this when I was little."

"There are only so many rides you can go on when you're little," Devlyn reminded him. "Grandpa kept you fairly close to the little-kid rides and attractions so he wouldn't have to say no to anything. He didn't like saying no to you. Or me."

"He loved us."

She ruffled his hair. "He sure did. Thirty minutes. Then we've got to go."

"So soon?" He aimed a look of classic disappointment at her, then Rye, imploring.

"School tomorrow."

"But we'll come back another time," Rye promised. "I bought season passes. That way we can come whenever we want."

"Anytime? For real?"

"Any time that works for the hardworking adults in your life," she told him, then tapped her wrist as if wearing a watch. "Thirty minutes. Make the most of it."

"Blazing Fury! Come on, guys! Let's go!"

They'd ridden the roller coaster twice already, but lines were nonexistent on a Sunday evening this early in the season, and if that was how Jed wanted to spend his last thirty minutes at the park, so be it.

They rode the Fury three more times, then managed one more coaster ride before Devlyn called it a day.

She hated to disappoint Jed, but it was a school night. "Guys. It's time."

Jed didn't get upset.

Instead he threw his arms around Rye. "Thanks, Dad! Thanks so much! This was like the best weekend ever!"

Dad.

She lifted her gaze to Rye's as he gripped their son.

He grinned, delighted. And winked at her. "It sure was, Jed. It sure was."

They'd come to Dollywood in Rye's car. On the way home, he handed her his phone. "I know your next two weeks are busy. Mine, too. I've got some important research to do before the town meeting. Miles is bound to throw up some roadblocks at that meeting, and I need to be ready. But can you jot down dinner with Dev and Jed every night in my calendar?" He flashed a grin her way. "Because I'll smile every time I see that reminder come up in my phone."

"Happy to." She set the reminder for each day, then put the phone down. "Of course, the nights I'm working at the store, it might be just the two of you, but that's kind of nice, too."

"Yeah." Rye flashed a smile back to Jed through the rearview mirror. "Yeah, it is."

Flowers.

Candy.

Quiet walks in the sweet spring air once Jed went to sleep. Occasional kisses.

Rye was courting her. He hadn't said as much, but it was there in his voice. His words. His kind gestures and his humor.

And she was loving every minute of it.

"You folks have been having a lot of suppers together," noted Biddy the following week. "It's kind of nice, getting to know one another again, I expect."

"Maybe too nice," Devlyn confessed. "Fool me once, shame on you. Fool me twice, shame on me."

"There's good sense in that, but there's truth in trustin' the Lord's way, too. Takin' hold of the path and walking straight and true."

"I believe that, but I can't shrug off the veil of caution," admitted Devlyn. "I understand why Rye made the choices he did, but there's a niggle of worry. And that's not good, because how can you love someone if you don't trust them?"

"We love them for who they are. Not what they've done. Or what they haven't done. But then we have to decide if we can deal with that," Biddy replied with her typical wisdom. "We love folks through their mistakes as best we can. But living with them? Well, that's a different conversation."

Her words struck a chord with Devlyn. She hadn't been willing to take a lot of chances the past ten years. Partly because she was a single mom, and partly because she'd been living with her parents. The thought of stepping out on her own with the business had seemed like an impossibility then.

Now it loomed, even though they'd lost so much. Of course, having the Smoky Mountain Development down payment in her bank account boosted her confidence, but she'd stepped out before Rye came on the scene, so maybe adversity had strengthened her.

Or left you little choice.

The little voice wasn't wrong. Maybe having her equilibrium shaken up wasn't a bad thing. The store was nearing its grand opening, Rye was amazing, and Jed was getting to know his dad.

Who could ask for more?

Just then, her phone rang. She saw Rye's

name pop up on the screen and answered it quickly. "Hey there. What's up?"

"I've got to head to Knoxville and meet with Roseanne and our legal team first thing tomorrow. I'll be back in time to have supper, but I'll grab it from Hidey's, okay? That way you can keep working. Sound good?"

"It sounds wonderful. Thank you."

"My pleasure, ma'am. Gotta run. Meeting with the civil engineers to go over Phase One. See you later. Dev?"

"Yes?"

"I'm glad I'm here, Dev."

Her heart soared. "Me, too."

He hung up.

He hadn't said those three magic words, but she had told him they were going slow. And yet when she looked at him, she read the emotion clearly. It was there in his gaze. His smile. The way he'd take her hand in his. The way he teased her and Jed. The patience he took with their son.

He'd taken Jed fishing the past Saturday. They'd brought home two catfish and three walleyes. Rye had shown Jed how to clean their catch, and then they'd invited Biddy over for wood-roasted fish and corn bread pudding.

She'd had all day to work at the store because Jed was with his father. That was a concept she'd never considered.

She contacted several crafters to drop off their work, checked in with Jordan and Shane to make sure everything with the store and the apartment was on schedule, then went back to sewing. She'd connected with the broker in Gatlinburg. It wasn't practical to expect enough handmade goods for the store's opening, but she had every intention of making that a priority for the store's first anniversary.

She was planning ahead. And that was

a new option for Devlyn. An option that felt absolutely wonderful.

Roseanne shot Rye a look of concern the next morning when he downed two pills with a quick swallow of water. "Headache?"

"Nagging. Nothing horrible."

"The humidity always does it to me," she replied. "The lawyers will be here in half an hour. Let's do a quick brief with Bodie before they get here. Coffee?"

"Please." Rye opened his carrying case, but when he reached for a sheaf of papers he'd put into the side pocket, they weren't there. The pocket was empty. He stared at the case.

"Problem?" Roseanne set down a mug of fresh coffee.

"The contracts aren't here." He stared at the case. "Yet I remember putting them here."

"I have the copies you sent." Roseanne shrugged. "No big deal. I'll have Carleen print them up. Bodie will join us in a minute."

Roseanne was right. It wasn't a big deal, except that Rye was never unprepared. He'd reviewed each deal the night before, double-checking himself. Had he left them in the cabin?

Bodie came into the small conference room just then. The firm worked out of a renovated house. The conference room had been the home's dining room at one time. The house was a prudent choice to build their growing business. Former bedrooms were now upstairs offices and the downstairs allowed space for meetings with clients and prospective buyers. Notes on their projects lined the walls of the spacious room with past, current and future developments. On the wall opposite his chair was the prospected outline of Kendrick Ridge.

"Hey." Bodie settled into a seat on Rye's right. He laid out a set of papers, handed Rye a set and put a third copy in front of Roseanne's chair.

She joined them and took her seat quickly. "Carleen will have those contracts printed up in just a few minutes, Rye."

"Thanks." Discomfort climbed his neck. He shrugged it off to focus on the present. Everyone made mistakes. It shouldn't be a big deal. And he did have a couple of wonderful distractions living next door. He'd never had to deal with that before.

That reality made him smile.

He'd spent more time focusing on Devlyn and Jed the past couple of weeks, and he wasn't sorry about that. In the end, they were just papers. No more. No less.

They shared figures and thoughts, and when the legal team arrived, they were able to finesse some details. From this moment on, the Kendrick Ridge concept had been fine-tuned into the reality it would be. Roseanne signed off with the law group, then slid the documents his way.

Rye pulled his favorite pen from his chest pocket and started to sign.

His hand shook.

He stared down, willing his hand to stop.

It didn't. Wouldn't.

It wasn't a major tremor. He was able to sign the papers no problem, but it wasn't the tremor that gut-punched him.

It was the combination of the headache, the missing papers he thought he'd put into the case and the tremor.

Fear snaked a cold hand up his back.

Stress, he reasoned.

The stress of being a dad, of reuniting with Devlyn, of being pulled in multiple directions when all he'd had to worry about for a decade was work.

They sent the legal team off and he stopped by Bodie's office just after lunch. A lunch he ignored because he wanted to get back north to Kendrick

Creek in time to bring supper. "Bodie, can you scope out possible options for land adjacent to the current plan? I want to see what else might be available in the next few years. Conrad's anxious to sell, but he wants a lot of money for short road frontage. And he's determined to make trouble. One thing I hate is rewarding trouble."

"His property was a major part of Plan B, wasn't it?"

Rye nodded. "It was and could be part of Phase Two now that we have the upper land secured for Phase One, but let's leave that alone until we have a sufficient income stream from Phase One. That gives us time to look around."

Bodie set the layout for Phase Two aside. "I'll check them out. Will the town be open to expansion?"

It was a good question. Kendrick Creek hadn't been able to agree on town goals for years. The mood was different now. More cohesive. Somehow the tragedy of the fire had helped bring people together. "They haven't always been so open to change, but the town's renovation following the fire is impressive. There's a lot of local investment going into it. These days a thirty-minute drive to the bigger towns is nothing. And you can't get prettier than being tucked on a rise in the Smokies. If you stand on the top of this knoll—" he pointed to Devlyn's land on their schematic "—the hills roll across the valley to meet the mountains on the other side. Once those lots sell, we automatically double our money. We were fortunate to get that parcel."

"So the higher price pays off in the end?" asked Bodie.

"Yes." A dull pain settled in behind his left ear. He held back a wince. "The town has made it clear to me that they like the idea of a community on Kendrick Mills Road, but not a fancy one. And we're okay with that."

He popped two more pain pills midafternoon. By the time he made the turn onto Route 411, his head felt better. Not right. But better.

As he drew closer toward Kendrick Creek a quarter hour later, his hand went numb. For a moment, he couldn't feel his hand gripping the wheel.

He could see it.

But he couldn't feel it.

The tremor began again. Both hands held the wheel, but his right hand moved on its own. He tried to stop it.

Nothing happened.

He gripped tighter.

That simply pushed the movement up his arm. His elbow quivered.

He stared at his arm, then pulled onto the road's shoulder. Parked. And when he released his grip on the wheel, his hand shook. Not badly. Not painful. But not controlled, either.

Stunning reality took hold of his brain.

He knew the signs. He'd studied them long before. He'd gotten through ten years of fine-tuning a business, building communities, giving people lovely places to live, work or play, and now he was on the cusp of doing the same thing in his hometown. He was on the edge of a beautiful life with an amazing son and being reunited with the love of his life, and yet—

Suddenly the tremor slowed.

Then it stopped.

Not bad. Not yet. But it was enough. Enough for him to know that the nightmare was at hand.

He couldn't stop it. He couldn't change it. But he could do the one thing that was hardest and perhaps the most helpful of all.

He could back away from Devlyn.

His heart crashed. His breath caught. A thrust of anger so immense that he wasn't sure how to contain it rose within him.

He'd been so close to a dream he'd never dared consider. Close to the gold ring every kid wanted on every carousel ride. Close to happy. Truly happy.

And now he needed to step away. Not harshly. He wouldn't do that to his son, but he needed to create a distance with the boy's mother, and that would be nearly impossible when all he wanted to do was get closer. Be the man she'd thought he was years ago. Be the husband and father she and Jed deserved.

But that would never happen now. He couldn't walk away in fear. Not this time.

But he could back away, and that would be even harder.

Devlyn spotted Rye's car pulling into the cabin yard and hurried out to meet him. "Did you get my message? That Jed was eating at Shane's tonight with Jolie and Sam?"

He shook his head as he climbed out of the car. "Sorry. Had my phone off during the meetings and forgot to turn it back on. We'll have leftovers for tomorrow, then." He handed her two of the boxed dinners.

She breathed in the rich scent of barbecue and smiled. "I skipped lunch, so this is particularly special tonight. Thank you, Rye. I'm still knee-deep in work over here. Can we eat in your cabin? So I won't have to put the sewing away."

"Can I get a rain check?" The question sounded casual.

It wasn't. When she met his gaze, he looked anything but casual. He looked distracted. "Of course. Is there a problem? Anything I can help with?"

"I've got some things to take care of. It's crunch time for the proposal's approval and I don't want to take anything for granted. I need to refocus my energies on work."

A niggle of guilt tweaked her. "Have we been taking up too much of your time?"

"No." He sounded sincere, but she read

the look in his eyes. Different. Almost… sad. "You guys are wonderful. But for now—"

"Work first. I get it." She took a step back and smiled at him. He'd been spending hours each day with them. She'd never really considered that he might be undermining his job. "If there's anything I can do to help, let me know, okay?"

"I will. Thanks."

He didn't kiss her goodbye.

He didn't grasp her hand.

He barely met her eyes.

He turned and walked into his cabin without a backward glance, and when the door closed, she felt left out.

She pulled out her phone and called Biddy. "Hey, I've got Hidey's BBQ here and no one to share it with. Have you eaten?"

"I've had a bite, but I can stand another. Come on down."

She crossed the grass. Biddy was waiting at the door. She swung it open with a smile. "What a nice surprise!"

"Jed's with Shane's kids and Rye has to work, so you're doing me a favor by having supper with me."

"It's the other way round." Biddy led the way to her small kitchen. "I've got renters coming in first thing, so I've been busy getting things ready. A hot meal will be a treat."

Biddy was right. Grabbing takeout hadn't been part of Devlyn's budget in a long time, so a full serving from Hidey's was a gift.

An hour later, Jess drove in to drop Jed off as Devlyn crossed the grass. Her son hopped out of the car and made a beeline for Rye's porch. "I'm goin' next door, okay?"

Before she could advise against it, Jed was at Rye's door. He knocked hard.

Rye opened the door as Jess came around the hood of her car. He smiled down at Jed, then pushed the screen door open. "Hey, guy. You're home?"

"Yeah." Jed gazed up, excited. "I got a B+ on my essay thing and I got a hundred on my math test. It's easy, like you told me," he bragged to his father. "There's only one right answer, and if you check your work, you'll always be able to get it. So I did what you said and it worked!"

"Well done." Rye hugged him.

He didn't look up. Didn't seek Devlyn's smile or attention. And when Jed asked him to have a quick catch with a football, Rye seemed regretful. "I can't, pal. Not tonight. I've got a bunch of work to catch up on. Tomorrow, okay?"

"Oh, well, yeah. Sure. If you've got work and stuff." The sincerity of Jed's acceptance touched Devlyn's heart.

It seemed to touch Rye, too. He glanced toward the yard, as if reconsidering his refusal, then took a breath and stepped back. "See you tomorrow, Jed."

"First thing," Jed replied before he dashed down the stairs.

Rye looked at Devlyn now, but it was a different expression. A little distant. He didn't say anything. He acknowledged her and Jess, then went back inside and shut the cabin door.

"It's nearly sixty degrees out and yet there's frost in the air," mused Jess. She shot a look toward Rye's cabin. "Wait—no. It's your runs-hot-and-cold neighbor. What's up with that?" she whispered as Jed retrieved his backpack from her car.

"Stress? Work? Cold feet? Déjà vu all over again?" Devlyn kept her voice low as Jed went inside. "I have no idea."

"He has to present his plan to the town this week, doesn't he? With the adjustments the board requested?"

"Yes."

Jess cut him some slack. "That's got to be stressful. Miles has made no secret of the fact that he feels duped. And you know Miles. He's in it for himself. Always."

"Rye did say he's spent six months on this project, so there's a lot riding on it."

"Yes," Jess agreed, but Devlyn noticed the slight wrinkle in her brow. "I've got to get back. Mom wanted to play that pioneer game with Jolie and Sam, and I said I'd join in."

"How's she doing?"

Jess grimaced. "Not great. I notice the changes more and more each day."

Devlyn's chest went tight. "I'm sorry, Jess."

"Me, too. As much as I hated the wildfire, it was a blessing because it brought me back home. Gave me time with Mom, and I found Shane and the kids, so I'm grateful for all of that. And I get to share Mom's last months with her. Just working with her has been an eye-opener, Devlyn." She made a face of respect mixed with disbelief. "My mother has more wisdom in how she handles patients and life than I could have imagined. I keep wondering how I'm going to do it all when she's gone. Then I realize maybe that's why God has me here now. To listen and learn. To quote Granny Gee—'there's no such thing as too much learnin'. Just too much sittin'.'"

"That was Granny." Devlyn laughed. Granny Gee's plain talk had offered lifelong lessons. It was Granny who'd let Devlyn practice on her old sewing machine. Few women would have turned over their one working machine to an earnest ten-year-old, but Granny Gee had done it.

Jess headed out.

Devlyn zipped up her hoodie. The night air was chilling. She eyed Rye's door, then willed herself to walk back to her cabin.

He said he needed time to work. She had to trust that. Trust him. But as she slipped into her cabin, the thought of trusting Rye came with doubts.

She had no idea how to put those to rest, and that was a troubling truth.

stepped into her cabin, the thought of
sharing Rye come with doubts.
She had no idea how to put most to
rest, and that was a troubling truth

Chapter Fourteen

The dull ache in Rye's head didn't diminish overnight.

It worsened. He hadn't had a stress headache like this in years. He woke up after a broken night's sleep and felt weighted down. His head, his brain, his body, his spirit.

He'd walked into the cabin yesterday after making a lame excuse to Devlyn. He'd hated himself for doing that.

Then he stepped inside and realized why he'd done it. Why he had no choice. The sheaf of contracts was sitting on the table, in plain sight. He'd never put them into his bag.

He didn't make silly mistakes. He dotted *i*'s and crossed *t*'s, and double- and triple-checked details.

He crossed to the kitchen area to make coffee.

There was no coffee. The empty can sat there, mocking him. He'd used the last of it the day before and had intended to stop on the way home and grab coffee and bread.

No coffee.

No toast.

No appetite. But he did need coffee before seeing Jed off on the bus.

Forty-eight hours ago, he'd have gone next door and shared a cup with Devlyn. That was what he longed to do now. That was what felt right and good and perfect.

His fingers trembled as he reached for the door. Not hard, but enough. Numbness traveled from midarm to his hand.

His chest squeezed. It squeezed so tight that he wanted to beat on something. Break things. Scream at the sky or the wind or God or whoever it was that let things like this happen.

He'd messed up as a younger man. He saw that. Now he was on the cusp of joy, and the happiness he cast aside out of fear, only to have the fear realized.

Perfect timing?

There was no such thing.

God's timing?

He'd have said it made sense, but right now nothing made sense. Was the irony that he'd wasted the ten good years he had? Was that the lesson meant to be learned? Because if that was God's teaching, he wanted no part of it.

He strode out the door and went to the car. He didn't look left or right. He drove to the convenience store on the other side of town and bought an overpriced can of coffee, a loaf of bread and a reasonably priced cup of freshly brewed Colombian blend. His favorite.

His hand shook as he lifted the to-go cup to his mouth.

He ignored it.

He would forge on as best he could. There was no cure. No treatment. Nothing but an empty life of broken promises and an awful, early death. He'd work while he was able to and as hard as he could because, if nothing else, he'd leave Devlyn and their son a financial legacy that would keep them from ever needing a food line again.

And maybe, if things worked out, she'd find someone to love someday. It just wouldn't be him. He'd caused her enough grief already.

He managed to be busy the next two nights. He did it matter-of-factly, as if missing time with Devlyn and Jed wasn't that important.

He arranged in-person meetings with

the other planning board members, including the one whose farm did business dealings with the Feed & Seed. Rye understood undue influence, but he was determined to go into this meeting fully prepared, including a surprise for Miles Conrad. He hadn't liked bullies in grade school and he sure didn't like them now. It was time for Miles Conrad to be taken down a peg or two, and Rye might have the chance to do it.

He met with Shane Stone early in the day and walked into the Thursday-night meeting exuding confidence.

Inside, he was a wreck, but he shoved the wreckage into a back corner of his consciousness. He made his presentation with little problem, but Miles sat there, shoulders hunched, waiting for him to finish.

Then he grilled Rye.

He peppered him with a stream of questions, and when Rye answered each one, the collar on Conrad's shirt crept higher and the shop owner skewered the other two board members with a scorching look. It meant nothing to Hidey, but Rye saw the effect it had on the farmer.

Miles was in a position to mess with this man's bottom line. To adjust prices. Or refuse to carry a needed product or to buy from him. And he was the kind of guy to do it.

Shane Stone asked for the floor.

The clerk recognized him. He came up to the microphone and faced the board, but stood almost sideways so he could address the town, as well. "All y'all know what we've got going here now. That fire tap-danced its way through this town and across the valley, wrecking things. Homes burned. Folks got left with nothing. Some with less than nothing, owing money on things forever gone. This town faced a hard time. A tough time. But it didn't let go of its belief that good could come from bad. That faith moves mountains. And that good folks help one another. And we've done that. Exactly that. The new town center, the rebuilt church, sidewalks that have just been poured. And y'all know that big empty building on the highway, just north of town. Where Hidey's got his barbecue stand set up." He waited while folks nodded.

Then he raised a manila folder. "I've got a signed contract from Ag Supply that says they're going to refurbish that old warehouse and turn it into their first Eastern Tennessee location. Their store should be up and running by June first, which means growth and competition for our town, and I find that those two things keep prices and people in check." He directed a quick look at the farmer on the board. "Healthy competition is good for all of us. I don't know anyone who wants to make the drive to Newport every time they need to replace a broken tractor part or place a ten-thousand-dollar seed order." He lifted the envelope slightly. "Just thought y'all would like an update on what's coming our way."

Conrad half rose out of his chair. "You get approval on that, Stone?"

Shane shrugged. "Not needed. Already zoned for commercial business. And they're putting one of those farm sheds with the carryout front so Hidey can keep his barbecue going right there on the main drag, on the premises. Their financial officer thought it was smart to work together, and who doesn't love good barbecue?"

Murmurs of approval rounded the room, but more important, at least to Rye, was the farmer's change of expression. And when the supervisor asked for the planning board's vote, the three men voted. Hidey and the farmer voted to approve Rye's amended proposal.

Conrad's vote came last.

He hesitated. Stared at Rye. Then he blinked, and when he did, Rye knew he'd won.

Conrad voted yes, not because he liked the proposal or Rye, but he wasn't stupid. His land would be optioned for Phase Two, and if he didn't start playing nice, folks were about to have an alternative place to shop for farm, ranch and outdoor supplies.

They'd bested him. That felt good.

Their beautiful community would be a blessing to this town, but the success didn't soften the recent blow to his personal life.

The supervisor called a ten-minute recess. When they reconvened, he called a vote for full town approval, and just like that, it was done.

"Mr. Bauer, the town of Kendrick Creek gives unanimous approval to your revised proposal for the over-fifty-five subdivision labeled 'Kendrick Ridge,' spanning frontage on Kendrick Mills Road and County Line Road as written. Congratulations."

Done. With Devlyn's parcel and his

grandparents' farm. That made this deal financially and emotionally sweet. Grandmaw would have been the first to congratulate him and welcome new folks to town. And Devlyn—

The balance of the seventy-five thousand dollars would give her enough money in the bank to be comfortable until the store was able to pay the bills. He wasn't sure how many pillow covers a person had to create to make a living, but he was pretty certain it was a lot.

The town board came forward and offered their hands in thanks.

Rye shook each one in turn, but when he looked around the room, the most important people weren't there. Jed and Devlyn were nowhere to be seen.

He'd wanted them there. He wanted Jed to see his father's moment of satisfaction for a job well done. He wanted Devlyn's approval. Her winning smile.

But he couldn't invite them and keep

his distance, so he'd left them out of the equation.

It was already hard enough. Living next door to Devlyn and being nothing more than civil tore at him. She didn't know that he was protecting her.

You did this before, his conscience chided. *How'd that work out for you?*

He lifted a bottle of water to his lips. His hand trembled unexpectedly and water sloshed from the opening, onto his shirt and jacket.

No one seemed to think anything of it. Doc Bristol and Jess were there. Doc handed him a napkin casually, then posed a question about his mother. "I heard your mom was in town a couple of weeks ago."

He nodded as he swiped the napkin across his collar and the upper front of his shirt. The movements weren't smooth, like they should be, but he got the job done. "I wanted her to meet Jed."

"Of course." Doc smiled at him. She

was fighting an incurable form of brain cancer and she was on borrowed time, but her smile was sincere even though her eyes seemed worn. "If she comes to town again, let me know, won't you? I'd love to see her. She and my mother worked together to do all the laundry and gowns for the clinic when I first started it over forty years ago."

"I didn't know that. I knew she made things and washed things."

"That's an understatement," Mary Bristol told him. "She was working full-time, you were just a little tyke, and she wanted some extra money to make ends meet, but it had to be something she could do at home. I'm glad things have worked out well for her."

"Me, too."

One of the council members approached Mary.

Rye backed away.

Jess was beside her mother, talking and smiling as if everything was all right.

But it wasn't. Her mother was dying. How could they act so normal? Was it easier to face death at seventy than at fifty?

He crossed to the door. It stuck when he turned the handle. He gave it a good push. It popped open and the outdoor air hit him full in the face. It felt good and bad all at once, like his life this week. How much could one person take?

The quiet of the night surrounded him. The chilled air felt good, too, like a wake-up call, except he was pretty sure he'd stepped into a nightmare days ago and simply couldn't wake up. Mostly because it wasn't a dream. It was dreadfully real.

He was proud that the plan was approved. But that joy meant little compared to what he'd lost.

Look what you've gained, his conscience chided. *You have a son you didn't even know existed. He's wonderful. His mother is a marvelous woman. Maybe it's time to count the upside. Count your blessings. Stop waiting for doom.*

He kicked a tire of his fancy car, then kicked it again because the first time felt that good.

His brain knew nothing. Less than nothing. Yeah, maybe he ran scared too early, but news flash! The worst-case scenario had come true at the worst possible time.

If he had to blaze a quiet trail forward to make sure Devlyn and Jed were taken care of, he'd do it. But he wasn't going to put them through what Aunt Mae had faced. Devlyn didn't deserve that. Jed didn't need to see it.

He drove back to the cabins.

The sun set later these days, but chill descended quickly when the western mountains shadowed those last rays.

Biddy's house was dark.

Devlyn's cabin was lit from within. The light beckoned him. Her spirit called to him. How easy it would be to head over there, and just be the man he could be for her. Play the role until his condition made it impossible. He hated denying himself that chance.

But the other option laid it all on them, which made it no option at all.

Chapter Fifteen

Morning sun stretched long golden fingers of warmth across the valley on Saturday morning.

Rose vines climbed higher on the trellises. Spring bulbs were fading, but dahlias were filling in nicely, and beyond them, Biddy had black-eyed Susans and coneflowers standing tall. They'd blossom in a few weeks, adding their pinks and golds to a parade of early color. The change suggested the rebirth of hope across the fire-scarred valley.

Shane Stone came by the cabins midday. Devlyn had the inner door open, letting fresh, warm air fill the cabin. Shane bounded up the steps like he always did and dangled a set of keys. "Your store and your apartment are ready. You can move in anytime."

Such good news. Whatever was going on with Rye, she could benefit from putting some distance between them. Being ignored while living next door didn't cut it. She accepted the keys. "Can I borrow one of your trucks to move my stuff? There's not a lot, but it won't fit in my car."

"There's this, too." He handed her a gift card. To a Sevierville furniture store. "Everyone knows you lost all of your furniture in the fire, Devlyn, so here's a little something to help you get the apartment set up."

The gift card was marked for five thousand dollars.

She stared at it.

Quick tears smarted her eyes. Her jaw quivered, and she did not want to ugly cry in front of Shane, but when she met his gaze, she did exactly that.

He reached out and gave her a hug. "We've got a great town here, Devlyn. I'm glad I came back to realize that."

"I can't accept this."

"Can and will," he said cheerfully. "There's no giving it back. And the store said that if you picked things in stock, they'd deliver by Monday."

Monday was when they'd open the doors of the new store for the soft opening. The grand opening was scheduled for the following Friday, but it was always wise to test systems first. "Talk about a busy day."

"If you're all right with it, we can get you moved out of here and set up in the apartment while you're working at the store. Which looks great, by the way."

"That's Jordan's doing." Jordan had taken on the task of putting things into place as they arrived.

"She's got a talent for it, but you ordered the goods. It's real pretty. My bride can't wait to be your first customer."

She stretched the gift card toward him. "Shane, take this back. Please. I can't accept this."

"Sorry." He stepped back. "No can do. And that stuff looks great." He motioned to the couch filled with stacks of pillows, throws and curtains. "As we get moving on building here, Devlyn, I'd like to use you to stage the model homes. It's a ways off because we have to finish the fire-damaged buildings first, but staging a model home is key to sales."

Staging homes.

How could one part of her life be taking off so perfectly while another part was fading into oblivion?

Her chest pinched tight beneath the smile she offered Shane. "I would love that. It's an honor to be asked, Shane."

"Our pleasure, ma'am." He tipped a finger to his Stonefield Construction cap and went back to his car.

She hadn't seen Rye this morning. She hadn't seen him except in passing for days. He'd played catch with Jed, and when Jed had innocently invited him over for supper the night before, Rye had graciously refused.

"I've got to finish things up, son."

"But Mom said the town told you that everything is all right now." Jed had gazed up at his father, confused. "So can't you just have supper with us? Please?"

"Yes, the town approved our project, so that's great." Rye had put a hand on Jed's shoulder. "But I have to make sure everything is lined up for the neighborhood to take shape. I won't always be this busy, Jed."

She'd heard their conversation through the open door.

"But I will be for a little while. And didn't you say that baseball practice would be starting soon?"

She hadn't heard Jed's reply, but she'd

heard Rye's. "Then let's move over to the gravel. I'll lob you some grounders and bounced balls. Time to get back into practice."

Jed hadn't said anything about Rye's refusal when he came in.

She hadn't, either.

She shoved aside her worn, foolish heart, and when Jed was tucked in for the night, she spent another ninety minutes sewing.

She didn't need a blossoming romance to create beautiful things. She'd proved that over the past decade. What she needed was a great work ethic and an entrepreneurial spirit, and with the grace of God, she had both of those.

As long as he was kind to Jed, she'd deal with whatever came her way. Like she always had.

Fool me once, shame on you. Fool me twice...

The old adage had come to pass, but

she pushed the concern aside purposely on Monday morning.

If wisdom was gained through experience, she should have been way smarter than she'd been the last few weeks. On the plus side, Jed knew his father and Rye knew him. And already loved him. That was something to be grateful for.

She hurried to meet Jess and Jordan in town. Her heart raced. Her hands were clammy. Nerves spiked a clench in her gut. She parked in the new parking lot behind the store and took a deep breath when she rounded the corner of the building.

Hers. All hers. A new day and a new opportunity.

She stared at the beautiful window presentation they'd finished late Saturday, and the inviting displays within. Devlyn's Knit & Stitch was the culmination of years of dreams, a chance she never thought she'd have.

She had it now. The prospect had

emerged from the ashes of tragedy, and gratitude filled her heart.

"Devlyn!" Jordan called her name from up the street. She and Jess had promised to meet her for last-minute run-throughs before they opened the door today. The sun had risen above the Smokies. It filtered through the famous mist that earned the Blue Ridge its name. The moisture would evaporate as the sun's rays drove temperatures up, and the warmth of the sun felt good.

"Are we ready?" asked Jess as she and Jordan stepped up on the curb edging the new sidewalks.

"The store's stocked, Jed's on the bus and I brought coffee for the brewing system. What more could we need?"

"Chocolate." Jordan's expression said that was a given.

"Supplied." Jess raised a box of decadent chocolate. "A gift from my husband, who actually thinks ahead. But I'm willing to take credit for it."

"Smart and beautiful. Shane Stone knew what he was doing when he snagged you." Jordan pulled the door open once Devlyn calmed her fingers enough to turn the key in the lock.

They walked in.

Beautiful.

"A new apartment and a new store, all in the same week. Devlyn, I'm so happy for you." Jess slung an arm around Devlyn in a side hug. "This is amazing. That window seat display is an absolute invitation to buy all the pretty things."

"Total Devlyn," Jordan told her. "She told Shane she wanted a broad window seat here so that folks can see how things would look grouped together."

"Well, this window provides the opportunity." Jess picked up one of the appliquéd throw pillows and squeezed it. "Birds, trees, leaves, flowers. And so many colors, Devlyn. It's a breath of fresh air after a long gray winter."

"I think I've been planning this in

my head for years," Devlyn told them. "Never thinking it would really happen. But it did. Let's get the lights on. Check the register system."

"I'll be your first customer." Jess didn't put down the pillow. She grabbed two more. "These are perfect for the porch swing."

"And she's got more in the back, so I'll refill the display." Jordan winked at Jess. "Just in case you think you got an exclusive."

Just then, Biddy came in. She stopped inside the door and folded her arms around her middle. "I have never seen a prettier shop this side of the parkway strip, sweet thing. And probably not even there. I am so excited to have the Knit & Stitch right here on the main road. I can't even tell you how happy this makes me, Devlyn."

"She's crying." Jess lifted her brows high in pretend horror. "Biddy, stop that.

Stop it right now. No one cries alone in my presence, and we've got work to do."

"I can't help it. They're happy tears, and after all this time, a few happy tears are a good thing," Biddy told her. She pulled out a tissue and dabbed her eyes. "I look at this, and what I see is that little girl, pulled up to your grandma's table, Jess, and working Granny Gee's sewing machine."

"Biddy, darling, that was thirty-four years ago." Devlyn made a funny face. "I might be almost embarrassed that it took me thirty-four years to get to this point."

"Oh, please." Jordan rolled her eyes as she switched on the lights. "Every road has a few speed bumps and detours. That's just life, isn't it?"

Devlyn nodded.

"Sometimes a body has to go up to go down," said Biddy. She took her light sweater off and hung it on a hook near the stockroom at the back of the store.

"And those detours can take us down some pretty roads."

"And to unexpected destinations." Jess turned the coffeepot on. "When this is done brewing, we'll toast friendship, time, opportunities and second chances. Because who would have pictured us like this six months ago?"

Jess had been living in Manhattan and finishing her second round of chemo for breast cancer last fall. Jordan had been running the Friendly Dollar just up the road. And Devlyn had been tucked in her mother's house in the valley, barely getting by.

Then the fire swept down the mountain and took so much. But in its wake came a different normal. A new normal.

The door opened again.

Each time that little bell jangled, a part of Devlyn longed to see Rye come through that door. To laugh with her. Hug her. Congratulate her.

But it was Jess's mom who came in this

time. Doc Mary was carrying a plastic case, and Devlyn knew what it was before Mary had a chance to say a word. "Granny Gee's sewing machine!"

"The one and only. It's been tucked on a rack in my basement all these years." She walked the compact machine across the room. Shane had put a shelf up just behind the register. A shelf that was just the right size. Jess lifted the plastic cover from the machine, and she and Mary tucked it there, on the shelf, then stepped back. "Perfect." Mary aimed a smile at Devlyn.

"You don't want it for Jolie?" Devlyn asked.

Mary shook her head. "Jess and Shane can buy one for her. You can't re-create the history in this machine. How it launched a little girl's dream. Nope, this one stays here, on its shelf. Right where it belongs."

Emotion rose up.

Devlyn choked it back down. She hugged

each woman in turn, then swiped her sleeve to her eyes. "Thank you," she told them. The meager words weren't enough, but these women didn't expect a speech. They were here to drink coffee, eat chocolate and put the last finishing touches on the walls and displays. They were here out of love, and that longtime friendship made the simple thanks enough.

Grand Opening This Friday!

Rye was surrounded by news of Devlyn's new store.

Posters dotted the light poles and bulletin boards all over town. The biweekly local newspaper splashed a picture of the Knit & Stitch across its front page under a banner headline that read: Can't Keep Us Down! And because Smoky Mountain Development was staking Kendrick Creek with a sizable investment, Rye had started following the town's social media pages.

They were full of news of the new store

opening, sharing Devlyn's posts around half of Tennessee and part of North Carolina, tucked on the eastern side of the mountains.

He couldn't get away even by staying away.

Business had taken him to Knoxville midweek. He was gone two days and hated every minute of it. By the time he returned, Devlyn and Jed had moved out of the cabin, tourists with a yappy dog had moved in, and he was pretty sure the snippy dog's antics were going to drive him crazy.

A big *woof!* woke him Friday morning. It wasn't just Lou's deep-throated bark that interrupted Rye's sleep.It was the frantic yips and squeaks of rebuttal, coming from the unhinged dog living in the cabin next door.

Another series of deep woofs sounded, not far from his porch. Clearly Lou had come calling again, but he didn't sound quite right. He sounded anxious.

The small dog next door went ballistic. Her nails tap-danced against the front window of the neighboring cabin as she hopped, jumped and barked her fury.

Rye tugged his shoes on and dashed outdoors to see what was going on with Lou.

Lou raced his way. He came close and pulled on Rye's sleeve. The miniature dog's fury intensified, but Lou ignored the teapot-sized tempest. Locking eyes with Rye, he tried to draw him forward again.

"Hey. Let go. What's up, fella?"

The dog whined. Again, he tugged at Rye. Then he danced away, as if urging Rye to follow.

Light didn't break early on this side of the mountain. Dusky shadows and early-morning fog made following the dog a puzzle, but when Rye would fall behind, going around minor things like fencing and boulders that Lou scaled easily, the dog waited for him. Not patiently. Urgency darkened the shepherd's eyes and stance. But still he waited.

He didn't lead Rye to the house.

He led him to the former deputy's car. It was running. There was nothing unusual about that. Wayne ran it to warm it up on chilly mornings.

But Wayne wasn't in the car.

He lay prone about twenty feet from it. And he wasn't moving.

Kendrick Creek had been spreading news quickly long before social media came along. Jed had just been picked up by the school bus when Biddy texted Devlyn. Wayne went home to heaven this morning.

Devlyn called her instantly. "Biddy, what happened? He and Lou were just in town yesterday. I saw them walking along, just like Wayne did when I was a kid, as if he were still on patrol."

"I don't know. His heart, maybe. Or it was just his time, sweet girl. Lou came running for help. He broke through a screened window to do it, so he must have been watching his master go down. He grabbed hold of Rye and made him follow him back home, but it was too late."

Sadness deepened her friend's tone. "Oh, Biddy, I'm so sorry. I know he was a good friend to you and Bub."

Biddy's voice broke. "The best. A good neighbor and a good friend to both of us, and always there when we needed him. What will happen to Lou now? Such a good dog, but my insurance won't let me have a dog here, not with so many folks in and out of the cabins. And Lou's not a small fellow. He likes room to run. We can't let him go to the shelter." She paused and seemed to catch herself. "Well, now, sweet thing, I don't mean to darken your big day. We all have our time, don't we? Still, it stings to have it happen with no warning like that."

"Oh, Biddy, of course it does. And

what a good dog, to find help to try and save his master."

"And good help, too. Rye knows CPR. He tried to save Wayne. He never gave up on it even though it took some minutes for the EMTs to get there. I'd have lost breath. He didn't."

Rye had tried to save the old fellow's life.

That was wonderful, but it only made it harder to dislike Jed's father, because in truth, she couldn't dislike him. She couldn't even stop loving him, although she'd tried, and how pathetic was that?

He was picking Jed up from school today. She wasn't sure if Jed would hear about Wayne in school, but she didn't want his brain filled with misconceptions. She texted Rye a quick message. Can you explain to Jed about what happened to Wayne this morning? He liked the old guy and he loves that dog. He'll be worried.

She expected a thumbs-up. Or a positive emoji.

Her phone rang instead. Rye's number flashed in the display.

Her finger hovered above the accept icon. Other than a casual nod and essential information about Jed, they hadn't spoken more than a few words since that first night he chose to eat alone.

But she had texted him about something important. She took the call. "You got my message."

"Yes. And you're right—I know Jed liked him. I'm calling because I'm not sure what to say to Jed."

"What about a gentle version of the truth?" she suggested.

"I don't know that there is a gentle version when it comes to death."

That was a valid concern. "Do you want to skip picking him up? I can duck away from here for an hour and go get him. Jordan's here at the store to help. I don't want him hearing it randomly if we can help it, and if he takes the bus home, that's bound to happen. Jed's strong. He dealt with losing my dad and then my mother. But I'll pick him up if that's easier for you."

"I'll get him. We've got an errand to run. I can do this."

She wasn't sure if he was convincing himself or her, but he wanted the chance to be the parent and she needed to let that happen. "All right. I've got to go."

She didn't. Not really. There was over an hour before they officially opened the doors of the Knit & Stitch, and the soft open had gone smoothly. They'd been busy from Monday afternoon on, and that kept her and Jordan replenishing stock. She'd even had to put a rush on a reorder the night before. That felt good, knowing that people would come to shop at the store before tourist season took off.

"Of course. Goodbye."

The *goodbye* stung.

It was clipped. He hadn't softened it

with *see you later*, like normal people did when they were, in fact, going to see people later. Like when he brought their son by after school.

His loss. Not hers.

She refused to let her gullibility over-shadow a wonderful day, and when they greeted the stream of shoppers who were lined up for opening-day ten-percent-off coupons, she did it with a smile.

Chapter Sixteen

Rye didn't want to discuss death with his nine-year-old son. He'd had to deal with an unsteady hand and numbness multiple times the past few days, which was his own personal reminder of mortality.

But he was a dad now, so he dived in once they were on their way to Newport to pick up flowers for Devlyn and the new shop. "Jed, Deputy Wayne passed away this morning."

Jed shot him a sad look from his seat. "I know. They didn't talk about it in school, but Benny Smith has a phone and he saw it even though the school is supposed to be blocking the internet. I cried. Just a little," he added, as if admitting to tears was weak. "Mrs. Retzler let me go to the nurse's office and have some juice. How is Lou?"

"He's all right. He's staying with Biddy for a little while. He came and got me to help, but it was too late, Jed. I'm sorry I wasn't able to help more."

Jed's sad expression pierced Rye. What if he'd run right over at the first woof? What if he hadn't bothered with shoes? That minute and a half could have made a difference.

Are you really taking this on your shoulders? You want to undermine God's control? How's that been working out for you so far?

He didn't want to undermine God's control. He simply wanted to spare his son. He wanted to keep Jed's road smooth, well paved and user-friendly. Was that so wrong?

They picked up the floral arrangement a few minutes later. Jed's eyes went wide. "It's huge."

"Opening days are big deals."

"I know." Jed's reply had the honesty and earnestness of youth. "Mom's been scared and happy and excited and nervous all week, but she said we are so blessed to have this chance and have so many friends that believe in us. And even when things get messed up, she tries not to freak out. So that's good."

The boy's innocent words broadsided him.

Devlyn didn't freak out. He'd walked away from her when she was knee-deep in getting the store ready and raising a child and she didn't go off the deep end.

He did.

Shame cut deep.

Yes, his prognosis was grim, but for the second time, he'd run away instead of confronting it head-on.

His mother's words about running

scared came back to him. Was he protecting them from what they would face? Or himself from witnessing them face it?

Both.

The store was still busy. Not crowded like it had been when he drove by this morning, but there were several shoppers inside. He pulled into a vacant parking spot and got out of the car. He took the large arrangement from the back seat and handed it to Jed once they'd crossed the road. "Your turn."

"I've got it, Dad." Jed slipped his arms around the box locking the ceramic vase into place.

A jingling bell announced their arrival when he opened the glass-topped front door.

Devlyn turned to face them.

She looked beautiful. Wonderful. Captivating. Surrounded by the work of many hands, she was in her element. She glimpsed him first, but didn't react. Instead she dropped her gaze to Jed, hidden behind the big floral display. "What creature lurks behind these stunning flowers?" she asked, loudly enough for everyone to hear.

"It's me, Mom!"

"Jed!" She laughed and came forward, gushing over the flowers, then put them in a prominent spot just to the right of the cash register. "They're beautiful, gentlemen." She raised her gaze to Rye. "Thank you so much."

"The store's amazing." What he really wanted to say was that she was amazing and beautiful and that he was a first-class jerk.

"The work of many hands," she replied. She laughed and bent to Jed's level. The overhead lighting brightened her blond hair. "I shall cherish those flowers, Jed. And thank you for thinking of them."

"Well, Rye asked me the other day if it was a good idea, and I said it was a *great* idea and could I help pick out the flowers, and he said yeah, sure, so he called the flower place and the lady said yeah, you can tell me what you want and I'll do it. So I did."

"You have great taste and a wonderful eye for color," Devlyn told him.

"Rye picked the daisy things." Jed pointed out the attractive scattering of multitoned daisies throughout the arrangement. "He said they were your favorite, so the lady said she'd use them, too. That means the pink and white and yellow ones are special from him."

Rye put a hand on Jed's shoulder. "We both wanted it to be special. Because today is special."

"Thank you both." She smiled down at Jed before lifting her gaze to Rye. Her gaze wasn't cool. It wasn't flat. But it wasn't friendly, either, and why should it be? He'd messed with her heart because he didn't trust her to handle the truth.

"Can I stay, Mom? I can help carry people's stuff to their cars?"

"Is that okay with you, Rye?" She was polite, like she'd be with any old customer. They'd agreed that Friday night would be Rye's night because there were no school or bedtime restrictions on Friday nights.

Rye nodded. "Would you two like to grab some dinner when you close at eight?"

"I would." Jed crossed to the back room and slung his backpack on a hook just inside the open door. "I will be so hungry for pizza then."

"Pizza works for me." Rye shifted his attention to Devlyn. "Is that good for you?"

She shook her head and ruffled Jed's hair at the same time. "You guys go ahead and get pizza. Then you can bring Jed back. I'm going to straighten up here so I'm ready for tomorrow. Thanks for the offer, though."

She was playacting for Jed's sake. She did it well. That meant she'd had too much practice putting on a strong face for her son. Probably for her mother, too.

Awareness rose up.

His love could have changed all that for her, but that option was off the table now. "We'll bring you some."

"Maybe mozzarella sticks, Mom?"

"I'd love it."

She went back to her customers.

Jed went to help a woman carry two bags to her car.

Rye stood alone in the midst of the small crowd and it felt awful. His head throbbed. His hand went numb. And then it started to shake.

He couldn't stop it. He turned to leave. When he was walking, the natural movement helped disguise the tremor.

He raised his gaze as he reached the door.

Jordan was watching him.

Not just him. She was watching his arm, and when their eyes met, he read the compassion in her gaze.

She knew.

It was there in her sympathetic expression. He pushed through the door.

She followed.

He got about ten steps in before he turned. "I'm going to ask you to stay out of this."

She rolled her eyes. "As if."

"I'm serious, Jordan."

"Rye, you always were. We all knew you had success, success and more success splashed across your DNA. There was something about you that stood out, but I don't get why you don't just tell Devlyn. Let her decide how to proceed."

"That's only because you haven't seen how awful it gets." He motioned to her lightweight shirt. "You don't have a coat on. Get inside."

She didn't. She stayed right there in the cool night air and faced him. "I watched my father die of Alzheimer's," she told him softly. "The older-age variety. I know this is different in some ways, but it's alike in others, and, Rye, I can't tell you how hard it was. But also how beautiful."

"Right."

"I mean it." She took a step toward him. "Being able to take care of him and be with him was an honor. Yeah, it was tough. Ridiculously tough at times, but it gave us the chance to show our love, and that's not a bad thing. Is it? Tell her what's happening. Don't hang her out to dry again."

Clearly she knew about their past.

"At least give her the chance to help prepare Jed for whatever happens. You don't want to broadside a kid."

That sucker punched him.

She was right.

Whatever was happening to him should take second place to making it easier for Devlyn to help Jed.

"Go see Doc Mary."

He frowned.

"She'll be straight with you. It might

seem weird to talk to Jess, but Doc Mary has seen it all."

"I think she's got enough on her plate, Jordan."

"You know better than that."

She was right again. Doc Mary had worked hard for the people of the valley for a lot of years. She'd helped his mother and his grandparents innumerable times, and that tidbit she'd shared about his mom doing washing for the clinic? That was Mary Bristol at her finest. Helping people with a hand up. Not a handout.

"It's up to you, but I always find the more I know, the less scary things are. And Doc will know where to point you to find the best information. She never lets up." A trio of women walked into the store just then. Jordan moved that way. "Gotta get back to work. Think about it, at least. She's still doing morning office hours three days a week."

She didn't wait for him to agree. She

needed to be inside, helping Devlyn and the shop look good.

He had two hours before picking up his son.

Two hours to think with nothing to keep him busy.

The church light flickered on just then. The pastor had promised to keep the church lit and the door open so folks could stop in anytime. He knew that self-doubt and dismay didn't follow regular hours.

Rye circled the old hardware store and the former bakery. The church sat at the crossroad, tucked a little bit back. Soft yellow light poured from the windows in the gathering dusk. The days were longer now, but once the sun dipped behind the mountains to their west, dusk settled quickly.

He slipped into the church.

It was empty. He'd been in big Knoxville churches that echoed when empty.

This smaller version didn't. He appreciated that because there was something lonely about a church that echoed. As if it longed for people of faith to come by.

Golden light brightened the simple sanctuary. It spilled over the old oak pews and the fresh ivory paint. The fire damage had been repaired, and at six o'clock, the beautiful bells began playing above him.

The years away had muted them in his memory, but they rang from the tower now, just like they used to. The tender notes of "In the Garden" rang out above him in the slow, proper cadence he'd grown up singing with his mother and grandparents beside him.

I come to the garden alone...

He was alone. He'd felt alone for a long time, even when surrounded by people.

When the dew is still on the roses...

Devlyn's appreciation of the beautiful floral arrangement came back to him. So happy with simple things. So strong in her walk of faith and life. But she wasn't facing what he was.

She faced being pregnant and alone. Raising your son. Dealing with her mother's anger and disappointment. Setting up her own business and now re-creating it from the ashes of the fire. She's faced her trials openly.

Shame hit him, but the rolling notes of the beautiful hymn didn't let shame win.

Devlyn walked with her faith. Not beside it. Not as a casual observer. She owned it proudly and shared that belief with their son. So maybe if he wasn't a church-on-Sundays-only kind of guy... Maybe if he practiced living his faith instead of just talking about it... Maybe...

He pulled out his phone and dialed Doc Mary's number. It went to an answering service that wanted to know if this was an emergency.

"No. But I need an appointment, the

sooner the better. If you could let Doc know that, I'd be grateful."

"Sir, the appointment line opens at eight thirty tomorrow morning."

"I appreciate that. But if you could let her know. Please."

"I will."

He gave her his cell phone number, and when it rang five minutes later, he knew she'd called Mary. "Hey, Doc."

"Rye, it's nice to hear from you. Suzannah called and said you needed an appointment."

A mix of fear and strength grabbed his voice for just a moment. Then he swallowed hard. "Yes. As soon as you can fit me in."

"Do you need care now? Is this an emergency?"

"No, Doc. Nothing like that."

"I've got tomorrow at nine thirty open. Does that work?"

"It does. Thank you."

"Good." Her voice was still warm, still

a comfort despite what she was facing. He wanted that strength. That courage. "I'll see you then."

"All right."

He hung up the phone as the bells eased into another song. He didn't recognize this one. It didn't matter.

The music soothed him. Or maybe it was the phone call, taking action that calmed his soul. Either way, he'd made a step forward, and it felt good. And scary. He stood and turned to leave the cozy church.

"Fear not, for I am with you... I will strengthen you. I will uphold you."

The calligraphy sign above the back doors paraphrased the touching verse from Isaiah.

Fear not.

Rye couldn't say his fears were erased, but they were eased. Reaching out to Doc Mary meant facing his fears, but it also meant he wouldn't be alone. That maybe somewhere, somehow, there was a plan. That was something to be grateful for.

Devlyn's eyes strayed to the flowers as she locked up the store to go upstairs to her apartment.

Their beauty touched her. Above them to the left was the shelf with the humble sewing machine. It sat proudly in its place, a symbol of a little girl's love for fabric and a lifelong dream.

She moved around the building as a car slowed, then pulled into the parking lot behind the new storefronts. Jed hopped out and headed her way when he saw her. "We got you cheese sticks, Mom, because we both know you love them. And Rye even ordered them at the end, so they didn't sit there and get cold, so they'd be nice and hot for you, okay?"

She hugged him. "More than okay. I was regretting staying behind. I will thoroughly enjoy those cheese sticks.

Thank you." She kissed his head, then raised her eyes to Rye.

His gaze settled on her.

Differently now. Like it had a few weeks ago, but Devlyn didn't play hot-and-cold games. She didn't play games at all. She offered him a faint smile of gratitude as he handed her the to-go container. "This will hit the spot. Thanks for thinking of me."

"Gladly."

He was cordial.

Good for him. She could be cordial, too. "And I appreciate you taking Jed out for supper. I knew he was hungry, but he was too excited to run upstairs and grab food because people were quite generous with their tips tonight. They loved having a young person on hand to tote things to their cars."

"I made eight dollars in tips," Jed bragged. "And one lady said I was the best helper she ever had. Like ever," he stressed. "So that's pretty good."

"It's excellent." Rye reached out to ruffle Jed's hair, but Jed had other ideas. He turned quickly and grabbed his father in a hug that ended up being a group hug because he hadn't quite let go of Devlyn.

The awkward moment was a quick reminder of what she'd hoped for before Rye pulled back.

She moved to one side, away from the embrace. "We've got to call it a night, my friend," she told Jed. "I've got an early start tomorrow and you promised to help until Shane picks you up to play football with your school friends."

"I'll be up early," Jed promised.

She handed him the key, then called after him, "Brush your teeth, Jedediah."

"Promise!"

She started to follow him.

Rye called her name.

She didn't want to make things worse, but what was there to talk about in the chilled night air? Nothing, really. And she was tired. She turned halfway. "Thanks for taking him out for dinner. It was the perfect ending to a tough day. Did your talk about Wayne go all right? He didn't mention it at the store."

"It went fine. I took your suggestions and treated it as naturally as I could. He did all right with it, but he's worried about Lou."

"I know." She'd been thinking about that all day. "But I can't have a big active dog like Lou here in an apartment. There's nowhere to run free and no time to walk him properly. I'd take him in a heartbeat if I could, but someone will open their hearts and home to him, I'm sure. Kendrick Creek takes care of their own. Thanks again." She raised the cheese sticks slightly. "Good night."

"Good night, Dev."

She didn't turn back to wave.

She opened the door. The stairs to their new apartment rose up in front of her.

She mounted them, and when she heard the engine of his car, she breathed deep.

Loving Rye was like riding a Dollywood roller coaster. Up and down, in and out, weaving this way and that.

She liked coasters well enough, and life had its share of ups and downs, but she could do without the sharp left turns. Those seemed to be part of Rye's nature.

It would have been so wonderful if—

She stopped that train of thought as she let herself into the apartment.

There were no ifs. There was reality, pure and simple, and her life had been blessed in other ways these past few weeks. She had a professional dream come true downstairs. She had much to be grateful for. If life included some disappointments in the romance department, so be it.

She and Jed had done all right together. Rye might be a part of the current picture, but she'd handle that on a day-to-day basis. Where Rye was concerned, there didn't seem to be a long-term plan one could count on, and that was a lesson she'd learned well.

Chapter Seventeen

Doc Mary faced him with a frank expression on Tuesday morning. They'd met on Saturday, she'd ordered some tests that had been run Monday, and now she faced him across the scarred but polished desk that had seen decades of use. "It's not Alzheimer's, Rye."

He stared at her. Blinked. Then he stared again as he drew his eyebrows down. "Of course it is."

She sighed, removed her reading glasses and quietly polished them while giving him a dubious look. "Of course it's not, and it never ceases to amaze me how patients manage to self-diagnose the worst-case scenario only to find out something entirely different. To start with, Alzheimer's doesn't start with tremors and numbness."

He remembered the sight of his father and Aunt Mae's words. How he trembled and shook. "Doc, I don't mean to argue, but my dad's tremors were terrible when I saw him."

"Rye, you saw him at the end. And yes, there can be tremors and shaking or no movement at all. The brain is a curious thing and the disease probably follows the path of least resistance. In any case, Rye, it's not Alzheimer's. I can promise you that. You have a hematoma here." She brought up a digital picture on her laptop and turned it so he could see it. Then she pointed to an opaque spot. "It's not big, but significant enough to cause symptoms."

"A tumor?

She shook her head. "No, it's a bruising

that hasn't reconciled itself yet. Have you hit your head lately? Or ever? Sometimes an old concussion spot will—"

The ladder at B&B Cabins. "A few weeks ago, actually. The ladder tipped at Biddy's and I fell. My head banged a tree stump, but I didn't black out or anything. Just had a headache for a day and a tender spot on my scalp."

"Here?" She reached out and touched the exact spot he'd hit.

"Yes."

"I believe it healed outwardly but hasn't reconciled itself internally. It might need to be relieved by surgery in Knoxville. A surgeon goes in and removes the tissue causing pressure on the brain. Patient is healed and symptoms disappear."

He couldn't quite believe what he was hearing. "It's not Alzheimer's? You're sure?"

"I'm sure."

"And not a tumor?"

"No. I'd like to see if it goes away

on its own. Give it a week to see if the symptoms improve. The numbness and headache should ease up if it's being re-absorbed. In the meantime, I want you to see a specialist in Knoxville to confirm what I'm seeing," she added. "That way you've got your foot in the door if they need to intervene surgically."

Not Alzheimer's.

"Here's the number for the neurology team. Call them today and set up a consult. Tell the desk that Dr. Kingston wants you in ASAP."

It wasn't a regular weight that lifted from Rye's shoulders. It was more like a boulder. He stood. So did Doc Mary. And when she reached out a hand to shake his, it was the steady confirmation of the news she'd shared.

Doc Mary never pulled punches, even when she had to deliver bad news. Folks loved her because they knew that about her and respected it.

He was going to be all right.

He took a breath as she leveled a stern gaze his way. "Stop borrowing trouble, stop anticipating what you can't possibly know, and go live your life. That's my overall diagnosis, Rye Bauer."

Go live his life.

He hugged her.

Hugging wasn't quite proper, and he knew she had her own health issues staring her in the face, but she'd gone out of her way to meet him on a Saturday—

The fact that it was her day off hadn't even occurred to him until after their original appointment.

And she'd gotten the follow-through done quickly. Because she saw his worry and sought to relieve it.

He wasn't sure his feet even touched the ground as he strode out of the new medical offices Shane's crew had built for Mary and Jess after the fire.

He had things to do. Plans he'd abandoned because he'd let fear win again.

No more.

He got to his car and sat there, considering what his next steps were.

He needed to see Devlyn. He needed to explain what had happened, beg her forgiveness and see if she'd give him a second—

Make that *third* chance.

And if she would, he'd make it count. Not because he owed it to her. But because he loved her enough to make it happen and it was high time he made his love for her a priority.

Woo her.

The old-fashioned phrase hit like a light bulb moment.

Wooing was in order. Courting. Something sweet and good and nice and worthy of an amazing woman like Devlyn McCabe.

He called Roseanne the next morning. "Roseanne, listen, I'm going to stay here in Kendrick Creek a little longer. I'll commute back there as needed, but

I want to see this project off the ground from a closer vantage point."

"Rye, that sounds good to me." Rose-anne always looked at the common sense of the situation. "That location puts you closer to the area we've been eyeing for that assisted living facility north of Sevierville. I sent you a couple of prop-erties that might work for us there. I know you've got a personal stake in this, Rye," she added. "I respect that. The rea-son we've worked so hard to establish a ground floor was so we could keep building, right? The planning phase is your expertise. Selling and coordinating fall firmly into my column."

"That's why we make a good team. I'll check out the properties for the as-sisted living complex while I oversee the groundwork here."

"Let me know what you think, okay?"

"Will do." He disconnected that call, then called a local Realtor. Wooing an amazing woman like Devlyn wasn't a chocolates-and-roses kind of deal, although those had their place in a well-thought campaign.

With his track record, he needed a till-death-do-us-part plan of action, because the woman in question currently had no reason to believe he was in it for the long haul. He needed to convince her otherwise.

He kept his scheduled meeting with representatives of the local utility companies, then met the real estate agent in her small office north of town.

If there was one way to showcase staying power and intent, it was buying real estate, and Rye Bauer knew that better than anyone.

Spring in the valley wasn't just a season—it was a gift, Devlyn decided as she opened up the store on Thursday morning.

The tourist season swelled with the climbing temperatures, and the increased volume could make or break a fledgling business. The thought was unnerving, so she didn't let herself dwell on it. From this point on, she was all business, so when Rye stopped by midday, she made sure to put on her business face. The fact that he arrived bearing a fresh, hot mocha was of little consequence. He handed her the mocha as he opened the conversation.

"Can I have a few hours of your time on Monday?" he asked. "Would Jordan be able to handle things here?"

She set the mocha down. She'd been restocking yarns and kept right on doing it because, coffee or no coffee, she would stay focused on work. "What do you need me for?"

"Advice."

She rolled her eyes on purpose.

"I'm looking at properties."

That got her attention. She stopped loading Christmas Cranberry into its cubby and looked at him, still ignoring the enticing scent of the chocolate-laced coffee. "Another project?"

He splayed his hands. "I've been away for a long time. Local advice is key."

That was a pour-salt-in-the-wound kind of statement. She knew that better than anyone. She faced him, waiting.

"You know the pulse of the town. The people. What might work and what won't."

"I can tell you straight off you're rushing things, because you haven't broken ground on your first venture and folks around here like to be shown," she reminded him. "Words are a dime a dozen. Actions are what people like to see, and you haven't proved anything yet."

"Exactly why I need your advice," he answered decisively. "I've gotten where I am by paying attention to what's going on, so I don't want to be out of my element here, Dev. Listen, if you're too busy, I can—"

She interrupted because she'd promised herself she wouldn't be a jerk to him. She'd seen too many parents form opposing camps by drawing tough lines in the sand, and no kid deserved that. "Do you want to tell me more about the project?"

"Can we go over it on Monday?"

It seemed like a reasonable request, so she nodded.

"You'll want shoes or boots for the outdoors," he added.

"Will do. But bring coffee." Traipsing through damp spring acreage would go better with hot coffee.

"Gladly." He hesitated as if he were going to say more, then moved toward the door. "Am I okay to take Jed tomorrow night as planned? I'm not doing anything on Saturday and you're working, so is it all right if I hang out with him on Saturday, too?"

A father shouldn't have to beg for time

with his child. She agreed quickly. "He'd love that. I think some middle schoolers asked him about a pickup football game for Saturday afternoon again. I'll text you the info. And I'll make sure he has the extra clothes he needs."

"Thanks, Dev."

He left with a friendly wave.

That felt wrong on too many levels, because there was nothing casual about her feelings for him. Her problem. Not his. But she'd better get a handle on it, because planned or not, Rye was a permanent part of the picture now.

The store set a new sales record on Friday, then nearly doubled that on Saturday. The warmer, drier weather had folks coming out in droves, and not just tourists. Locals from across the valley used the gentler weather to check out the town's restoration.

She'd set shortened hours for Sunday, noon to five, and when she and Jordan left the store at five thirty Sunday evening, she'd had a glimpse of what a town storefront meant for business. It amazed her.

She locked the door and turned.

Jordan gave her a high five.

She took it, and for the first time since the fire, she felt like she could breathe. "People love this." She indicated the pretty shop with her eyes. "I hoped they would and they do. That's so gratifying, Jordan."

"Location, location, location," Jordan told her. "Discoverability is huge in marketing, here and online. And once you build a reputation, it spreads. You've done it." She reached out and they hugged each other. "You've arrived. And nobody handed it to you. You had help along the way, but that's just small-town friendly. You did it on your own, and I'm so proud of you."

Devlyn smiled, and as Jordan headed across the street to her car, Rye pulled up with Jed. She moved forward, puzzled as Jed hopped out of the car.

"Rye came to get me because Mary wasn't feeling good and I told Jess you were working and she should just call my dad. So she did."

He said it matter-of-factly. As if having a father had been a regular thing instead of a new reality.

Rye's smile deepened. "Glad to do it, bud." He faced her directly. "How about if the three of us head to Newport for supper? I'm in the mood for a good steak and I think we need to celebrate your shop's first week with a fancy supper. My treat."

"Like a whole steak?" Jed's eyes went round when he lifted his brows. "For me?"

"Think you can handle it?" asked Rye.

Jed laughed out loud.

"I would love it so much. I'm always hungry!"

That much was true. Feeding a growing boy was an ongoing task but no longer a struggle, and that was something to be grateful for. "I'm not dressed for a fancy restaurant," she told them, but Rye wouldn't let her wriggle her way out of it.

"The food is fancy. The place is country casual. Like us," he assured her, and something in his gaze, his voice, made her say yes when she probably should have said no.

But food sounded good, and food cooked and served by someone other than her sounded even better. "Give me fifteen minutes to wash up and change."

"I'll call and make a reservation."

She hurried upstairs and took the full fifteen minutes, glad she hadn't fallen behind on laundry. When she reappeared in a different outfit and freshened makeup, she pretended she didn't notice the light of appreciation in Rye's gaze.

But it felt nice to see, anyway.

They had a lovely dinner.

Jed hadn't been out to a steak house

since her parents' fortieth wedding anniversary dinner nearly six years ago. He'd needed a booster chair then.

Now the almost ten-year-old sat straight and tall. He didn't just enjoy his meal. He practically launched an attack on the steak and potatoes platter. He not only finished everything, he enjoyed a sundae for dessert.

He was growing up.

Mixed emotions stirred her. Seeing him with Rye and witnessing their growing rapport was good, but it also meant sharing, and she needed to get better at that.

When they got back to the apartment, Rye insisted on seeing them in.

She balked. "It's right there. The door. The stairway. We've got this, but thank you."

"A gentleman sees a lady in. It's how it's done, Dev."

Jed had gone on ahead. He'd unlocked the lower door and hurried up the stairs.

"Besides, I've got to say good-night to the kid."

And Jed needed to thank his father for the wonderful meal. She preceded Rye up the stairs, and when he stepped into the sparse apartment, the urge to make excuses swept over her. The secondhand couch, the old dining table and two mismatched chairs, the utility shelving filled with flats of material.

It was clean but austere, and when she turned his way, she caught his look of surprise. She shrugged it off. She had that nice gift card, but no time to spend it. "The decorator hasn't had time to play in the apartment as yet, but that's what winter's for."

"Nothing wrong with simple. Grandmaw would approve."

That made her smile. "Those gals held a lot of mountain wisdom between them. GeeGee. Grandmaw. Biddy."

"Hey, Dad!"

Her heart stopped as Jed hurried back

to the kitchen/living room combo. Hearing him call Rye "Dad," seeing the joy on his face, a joy that was echoed in his voice, didn't just feel good. It felt right.

"I wanted to show you this." Jed thrust his third-quarter report card into Rye's hand. "I did better in geography! And thanks for the great supper. It was, like, so good! The best."

He hugged Rye. Fiercely. And then he didn't wait to be told to get ready for bed. He just hustled off to do it.

"He's a great kid, Dev."

"He is. And he's growing up."

"The appetite was an indicator."

She laughed. "I'm expecting a major growth spurt any day now because he never stops eating."

"We're still good for tomorrow?"

She hadn't been able to get their morning meeting off her mind. "Rye, it might be better for you to find someone else to advise you. We don't want to muddy the lines we've drawn."

He had the nerve to agree, with a caveat. "You're right, of course. I'd do that, except it's only hours away and there's no one I can call on at the last minute."

He made a good point. She agreed and tried to shelve her reluctance. "All right. What time?"

"Nine thirty?"

"Where?"

"1413 Ramsey Cove Road."

"I'll be there."

"Good." He reached out and touched her hand lightly. "I appreciate it, Dev."

She hid her reaction to the gentle touch, as if it were nothing. "See you then."

He left.

No lingering glance, no teasing grin, no over-the-shoulder look to inspire those what-ifs that had gotten her into trouble before.

Just as well.

But when she tried to sleep, visions of Rye and Jed filled her head. Not in a bad way. A good way. Overall it was the realization that Jed was about to turn ten and that he'd be gone in less than a decade. Gone to college or to learn a trade, whatever he wanted.

And she'd be on her own.

But not alone, she reminded herself. She'd be surrounded by friends. A town full of people who cared, people who lived together, laughed together, worked and prayed together. And that wasn't a bad outlook at all.

In God's hands.

She'd gotten this far by trusting the Almighty. She'd travel the rest of the way doing the exact same thing.

Chapter Eighteen

Devlyn parked behind Rye's car the next morning. Ramsey Cove Road wound its way up and around one of the gentler rises dotting the valley floor. It wasn't an overly populated road. A few houses here and there, on a road overlooking the valley below.

A driveway rose up to her left, into a stand of mixed trees. Leaves danced in the light breeze. Their shade would be welcome as spring marched toward summer.

"Here you go, as promised." Rye approached her with a to-go cup of coffee.

The scent of chocolate drew her in as she brought it to her face and breathed deep.

"Lovely."

"Agreed." He wasn't looking at the coffee. He was looking at her.

She shifted her gaze upward. "So this is the property we're looking at?"

"One of them."

"There's more?"

He looked a little apologetic. "If needed. Is that all right?"

She bit back an argument because he'd jumped in to help Biddy multiple times. And with Jordan's help, she could spare some time. She nodded. "It's fine, actually."

"Good." He reached for her hand, then drew back. "Sorry. Off-limits. I forgot."

"I would have reminded you."

"Of course." She thought he smiled, but if he did, he hid it quickly. "This way." He led the way up the gravel drive, and when they got halfway up the slope, the drive turned. A cape-style log cabin stood framed by the rise of the hill and the trees. Three dormered windows offered views from upstairs, and a wide wraparound porch snugged the house into its hillside setting. The forested backdrop complemented the house, and the yard flowed downward toward the small grove she'd noted from the road.

"This is lovely, but how can you put a community here?"

"Community?"

"You said you had a project to go over with me."

"A different kind of a project," he told her as he moved forward. "I've looked at different places, but this one spoke to me."

She frowned. "I don't get it."

"I'll explain as we go." He pointed toward the yard. "We can go across the lawn. Watch your step."

"Will do."

They crossed the grass and climbed the wooden steps. She turned and had to swallow back her surprise at the view. "Rye. That's a gorgeous view, isn't it? Except for the part where the fire swept down." The path of destruction was clear from here, but already the new growth of leaves was easing the dark scar of the fire's wrath. It would take years to erase it fully, but the earth would heal itself. Below, the sheen of new lumber and the white sidewalks lining the town center gleamed in the bright morning sun. "You can see the town."

"Yes. And your shop."

The church spire was slightly to their right, but the house was high enough and the front had been cleared enough to offer a panoramic view of the town. She could see the scattered neighborhoods and farms, and the rope of Highway 321, snaking its way north and south. "It's beautiful, Rye. Gorgeous. But what does your firm have in mind? It would be a tragedy to mess up this view."

"You like the view?"

"Of course. Who wouldn't?"

"Check out the inside with me."

"This is someone's house. We can't."

"I have permission." He put a key into the lock and turned it, then eased the door open.

The inside was lovely.

Natural light poured in from multiple windows. Prismed wind chimes on the porch danced fairylike rainbows across the front room. "This is absolutely charming."

"Isn't it?"

"Yes, but what are you going to do with it?"

"Live in it."

That pronouncement stopped her in her tracks. "Live in it? As in live here? In Kendrick Creek?"

"It's only an hour to Knoxville and I only need to be there one or two days a week, so why not?"

She'd thought it would be easy to deal with losing him again because he'd be an hour away. Just enough distance to back-burner him.

But here? In town?

"Before you make any judgments, I have to tell you something."

She wasn't sure she wanted to hear anything he had to say, because he'd just made her life exponentially more difficult and he probably knew it. "Yes?"

She kept her voice cool.

"I didn't shrug you off without good reason."

She faced him square. "There's nothing you can say to make this right, Rye, and we both know it."

He reached for her hand. "Give me five minutes, and if you still want to walk out that door, I won't stop you."

She wanted to give him a smart-aleck reply and flounce out the door, but she forced herself to act mature. "All right." She sat.

So did he. Right next to her. Close enough that she could count the tiny gold highlights that rimmed his pupils and lightened his eyes.

"I took a fall at Biddy's when we were doing the roof."

She frowned.

"The ladder slipped. I crashed and managed to smack my head against a tree trunk."

"How did I not know this?"

"You weren't speaking to me at the time, and I brushed it off as no big deal because it wasn't. A few weeks later, I began having symptoms."

She drew her brows down tighter. "What kind of symptoms?"

"Headaches. Tremors in my right hand and arm. Numbness that made my right hand and arm immovable. And I forgot some things. Important things and simple things. It started out of the blue when I went to Knoxville and kept getting worse. All I could see were my father's last weeks. What it was like. What *he* was like. What Aunt Mae endured to care for him. I thought I was starting to show symptoms. I thought it was the Alzheimer's."

"Is it?"

"No." He shook his head and a ripple of relief shot through her. "It was from the fall. The bump on the head. But I spent weeks assuming I was developing symptoms, and it wasn't until I went to see Doc Mary that I found out it was something else all along. A bruise between my brain and my skull that seems to be going away on its own. And if it doesn't, there's a doctor in Knoxville who'll take care of it for me. But in the meantime, I ran scared because I'd fallen in love with you all over again. With Jed. With the thought of what we could have together as a family, and it was like life played the meanest trick ever. Waiting until we found each other again before smacking me down. I backed away because I was stupid, Dev."

She wasn't about to give him a free pass. "Yes, you were."

"And cowardly."

There she disagreed. "There's nothing wrong with protecting the people we care about."

"The ones we *love*," he told her.

She let that go. "The problem isn't in the possible prognosis, Rye. The problem is in the not sharing. The lack of trust. And yes, the fear of moving forward, because it's life. Anything can happen to any of us, but I'm not one to live in fear, Rye. It's not part of me. And that's twice you walked away without a backward glance, and once was too often." She started to stand.

He put a hand on her arm. "You said five minutes. I've got ninety seconds left."

"Talk quick."

"I love you."

She wasn't expecting that and couldn't hide her reaction.

"That's the crux of it, Dev. I'm not perfect, I'm about as flawed as they come, and yeah, I got scared this time because I had the most amazing and surprising opportunity come my way. A son I didn't know about. A beautiful boy raised by an amazing mother, and the thought that you loved me again—"

Still, she thought, but kept that to herself.

"—made me the happiest man on earth. So when the symptoms began, I felt like God was snatching that chance right out from under me. As if He were teaching me a lesson, and I didn't want to learn a stupid lesson. I wanted you. And Jed. And a house to come home to and maybe even some of those pillow things that people are buying like crazy.

"I got mad," he admitted. "I overreacted. And I want to apologize." He glanced at his watch and saw that his time was running out. "And I want you to forgive me and marry me and for us to raise Jed together. If you say yes."

He held up his watch as the five-minute timer played a bell-like version of "The Wedding March." Then he slipped off the couch and took a knee. "Dev, will you make me the happiest man in the world and marry me? Live in this house with me and Jed and Lou? Grow old with me?"

"I get the house *and* the dog?" She didn't think she could be happier, but giving the orphaned dog a home wasn't only good. It was perfect.

"And the swing, too." He motioned out the side window. Hanging from a thick-trunked white oak was the scarred and broken swing that had hung at her parents' home for as long as she could remember. Only it wasn't broken anymore. Stout rope held it in place, ready for a second chance for new adventures. "I didn't try to fix it up too much. I figured it was like us, Dev. It earned a few scars with time."

The swing. It had lain in the backyard broken when Bobby Ray had come to do demo. She'd assumed it became a casualty of the cleanup. It hadn't.

Her eyes filled. Not from the swing, exactly. But from the consideration he'd shown in trying to make things right.

"I knew you loved the view from your parents' house on the rise, so when I saw this house, overlooking the town and the shop, it seemed right. Lou needs a place to run and a boy to run beside him. Although if you don't love this one, we can keep looking, darling. If you'll have me, that is."

She stood.

So did he.

He reached into his pocket and withdrew an emerald-and-diamond ring, a beautiful ring, set in yellow gold. "You told me once that you loved emeralds."

She'd mentioned that ten long years ago. "You remembered."

"And if I ever don't remember, Dev." His gaze turned serious. "If things don't go well at any time, I want you to know that inside I will always love you. Cherish you. And trust you. Even if my memory goes south on me."

Trust was key. Trust, love, faith and forgiveness. The basic tenets of a good life. "Yes."

"Really?" His face lit up. He slipped the ring onto her outstretched hand and motioned around them. "I don't even have to show you the rest of the house to seal the deal?"

"I won't say no to a tour, but it's not the house I'm saying yes to, Rye. It's you. The love of my life. The rest is window dressing."

Then he kissed her.

He pulled her into his arms and kept her there a good long while, and when he was done kissing her, he didn't let go.

He held on as if she were the most important thing in the world to him, and this time, Devlyn was absolutely certain she was.

Epilogue

The June sun filled the church with natural light. Biddy fussed with Devlyn's veil while Jess adjusted the simple flowers of her bouquet. "I have to admit, these bouquets are lovely. And amazingly frugal."

Devlyn laughed. "I come by it honestly. When you overthink what to do with every penny, it becomes ingrained. And we decided all the money we save by having a simple wedding and reception will be used to help families in the area who are dealing with Alzheimer's. We're setting up a foundation to help give respite to caregivers."

"That servant's heart of yours is paying off, Devlyn." Biddy hugged her, being careful not to mess up the veil. "Rye Bauer is good people." She made the pronouncement as she stepped back to look over the veil Devlyn had made. Waist-length, it suited the simple gown she'd chosen. The older woman gave the veil and Devlyn an approving smile. "The minute he started lifting a hand to fix things around the cabins, I knew we had a keeper. It was just a case of him knowing it, too. And my sister Lindy is going to buy one of those first Kendrick Ridge homes. They're moving back here because the city's gotten too big and busy and she says she's ready for the peace of the mountains again. It's amazing how things go around."

"And come around," noted Devlyn.

A soft knock sounded at the door.

Rye stood there and his smile of appreciation made her pulse run faster. "I have a guy here who wanted to see his mother."

Jed peeked around the corner.

He looked nervous. He wasn't a spotlight kind of kid, so being his father's best man put him in an awkward position. She motioned him in. "What do you think? Do I clean up all right?"

Jed gave her an awkward grin. "You look beautiful, Mom." Then he hugged her.

She gave Rye a raised eyebrow over Jed's head.

Compassion showed in his face. His smile. But then he offered a reassuring wink. "I told him he's only got to face folks for a few minutes. After that, we'll be facing Pastor Bob. And that his job is to keep me from getting nervous."

Jed let go of Devlyn and looked over his shoulder. "Do you get nervous, too?"

"Yes. But if you're up there with me, we'll be fine, son. Just fine."

Jed squared his shoulders and stepped

away from his mother. "Sure. Because we're together."

"Exactly."

Jed recrossed the room to stand by his father's side.

They were a picture together. A picture she'd love and appreciate from this day forward, woven from a fabric of love.

Rye clapped a hand onto his son's shoulder. "We'll see you up front, okay?"

"Yes."

"And, Dev, you are absolutely right," he went on as they started to move. He glanced back over his shoulder and winked again. "You do clean up nice."

She laughed.

He'd ignored protocol to bring Jed back here to calm the boy's nerves and it had worked. Who could ask for more than a man who'd learned to put faith and family first?

And when the strains of "Love Grows Here" indicated her turn to walk down the aisle, she walked forward confidently.

She met Rye's gaze as she approached and smiled. Just for him.

And then she took her place by his side forever.

* * * * *

If you loved this story,
be sure to pick up the first
Kendrick Creek book
Rebuilding Her Life
And don't miss Ruth Logan Herne's
previous series Golden Grove

A Hopeful Harvest
Learning to Trust
Finding Her Christmas Family

Available now from Love Inspired!

Find more great reads at
www.LoveInspired.com.

Dear Reader,

I hope you loved this story!

I've written over sixty books. A couple of them have been about Alzheimer's disease because it affects so many families in so many ways. But this book isn't about Alzheimer's.

It's about fear. And control. And forgiveness.

Rye Bauer believed he left Devlyn McCabe ten years before because he didn't want to tie her down to the difficult demands of the disease, but he realizes now that he let fear—*not faith*—do the talking. He'd valued his success, but it was a hollow victory in so many ways. Seeing Jed and Devlyn put him on a new path.

Devlyn prided herself on honesty, but when her choice to leave Rye out of Jed's life becomes front and center, she sees the selfishness in that decision.

It's not easy to overcome fear. We see

that in Rye. We have a hint of nervousness in Jed. And we know that Devlyn's a fixer, that she puts things together to make the world a better and prettier place. She's perfect for them.

I loved writing this book and I love Kendrick Creek. The pandemic has kept me from doing my normal annual research trips, but fortunately, I was able to visit Pigeon Forge, Gatlinburg and Cosby just before shutdowns began. Tennessee is filled with the friendliest people on the planet.

Thank you for reading Devlyn and Rye's story! You know I love hearing from you. Friend me on Facebook, email me at loganherne@gmail.com—I'd love to add you to my newsletter list!—or stop by my website, ruthloganherne.com.

Sending you Tennessee blessings!
Ruthy